D0324346

LOADS OF CODES AND SECRET CIPHERS

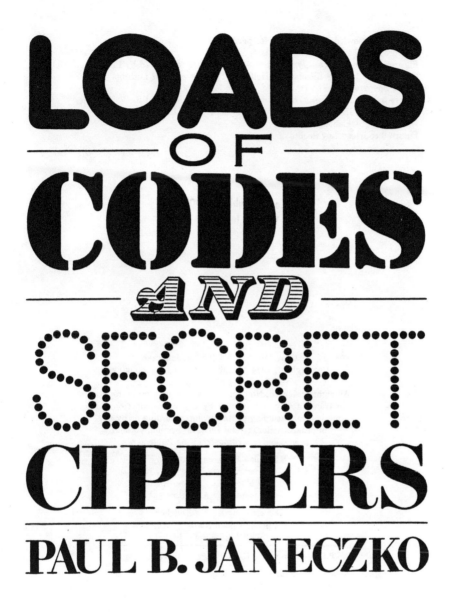

LOADS
OF
CODES
AND
SECRET
CIPHERS

PAUL B. JANECZKO

Macmillan Publishing Company
NEW YORK

Collier Macmillan Publishers
LONDON

Grateful acknowledgment is made for permission
to reproduce the following materials:
Figures 2, 5 and 6 from *Signs and Symbols Around the World* by Elizabeth S. Helfman.
Copyright © 1967 by Elizabeth S. Helfman. By permission of Lothrop,
Lee & Shepard Books (A Division of William Morrow);
Figure 3 from *The Manual of Brands and Marks* by Manfred R. Wolfenstine.
Copyright © 1979 by Manfred R. Wolfenstine. By permission of
University of Oklahoma Press;
Figure 9 courtesy Boy Scouts of America.

Macmillan Publishing Company
866 Third Avenue, New York, N.Y. 10022
Collier Macmillan Canada, Inc.
Designed by Al Cetta

Drawings by Kathie Kelleher
Printed in the United States of America
10 9 8 7 6 5 4 3 2 1

Library of Congress Cataloging in Publication Data

Janeczko, Paul B.
  Loads of codes and secret ciphers.

  Includes index.
  Summary: Discusses and provides practice in making
and breaking codes and ciphers, as well as in building
simple coding devices to transmit secret messages.
  1. Cryptography—Juvenile literature.   2. Ciphers—
Juvenile literature.   [1. Cryptography.   2. Ciphers]
I. Title.
Z103.3.J36 1984   001.54'36   84-5791
ISBN 0-02-747810-6

Special thanks to:
Barbara DeChristoforo,
who helped me start the book,
and
Beverly Reingold,
who showed me how to finish it.

With love and friendship
for Mary Belleville,
colleague and ally,
who didn't mind sharing
the stage with a gorilla.

Contents

Codebreaker. A sinister word that brings to mind pictures of spies in trench coats, foggy piers, and last-minute heroics. Yet the idea of codes and secret messages goes back over 2400 years to ancient Sparta, long before trench coats existed. Since that time, codes and ciphers have played an important part in the history of many nations.

But this isn't a history book about how other people used codes and ciphers in the past. That information is fascinating, but here it's included only to show you that the business of codes and ciphers is for real. The object of this book is to teach *you* how to make and send secret messages. I hope you will enjoy learning. The real fun will come, though, when you actually send a secret message and when you decipher one sent by a friend.

Here you will find everything you need to work with codes and ciphers: charts, plans, diagrams, messages, hints, and ideas. All you have to supply is imagination, clear thinking, and a lot of curiosity. You'll also need a notebook and a pencil. The notebook will be a place for you to practice writing secret messages and to jot down your own ideas. I've provided lots of messages to use for practice. And don't worry if you get stumped. The answers are at the end of every chapter.

Once you are writing and breaking secret messages, you might very well come up with new and exciting methods of sending them. If you do, I would love to hear about your methods. Just send me a letter in care of the publisher. I promise to answer.

Now, are you ready? Then get out your tattered trench coat, and let's enter the world of codes and ciphers.

Chapter 1
What's the Difference?
A Word about Codes

Just what *are* codes and ciphers? The answer is simple, even though a lot of people get the two mixed up or use one word when they really should use the other.

A *code* is a word or a group of letters that stands for another word or group of words. For example, the MAN-HATTAN ENGINEERING PROJECT was the code name for a project during World War II that produced the atomic bomb. The atomic bomb was referred to by several code names: THE GADGET, THE THING, THE BEAST.

In a *cipher*, on the other hand, each letter or number in the message represents another letter of what is called the *plaintext*. The plaintext is simply the message before it is put into code or cipher. For instance, NRAEL is a cipher for the plaintext LEARN, and 3-9-16-8-5-18 is a simple cipher for CIPHER.

Since every good code system is based on a code book, let's take a look at one such book. A code book is a two-column book that usually has two parts. You could think of a code book as a sort of foreign-language dictionary. In one half of the book, the uncoded words are arranged in alphabetical order in the left-hand column. The other column contains a code word for each word in the left-hand column. The second half of the book is exactly the opposite. The left-hand column contains the code words in alphabetical order, while the right-hand column contains the uncoded words.

Figure 1 shows a page from a real code book. I found this book tucked away in the dusty attic of a 150-year-old house I once lived in on the coast of Massachusetts. The book is *The International Code of Signals for the Use of All Nations.* It was not a wartime book, but it was distributed by the Bureau of Navigation of the U.S. Navy in 1890.

This particular code book is called a *one-part code book* because both columns are arranged in alphabetical order. With this organization, there is no need for a second part. Any coded or uncoded word can easily be found here.

It's not especially difficult to write your own code book. Of course, if you work with a friend, the project will take less time. You'll need some paper with a line drawn down the center of every page. A stenographer's pad, which can be found in any stationery or five-and-ten-cent store, would do nicely.

The best way to begin is to write down in the left-hand column all the words you think you might use in a secret message. Like what? Well, you could start with the names of people, places, and things in your neighborhood, your home, and your school. That should give you a hefty list right off the bat. Then you'll have to add numbers and the days of the week. Can you think of more words to include in your book? I'm sure you can, especially if you and your friend put your heads together.

Once this part of the code book is complete, you must then fill in the right-hand column. There are two ways to do this. One is to assign real words for your code words. Just make

CKNJ	AWASH.
CKNL	AWAY.
	Could any vessel have got away after you? . . . . HQF
	Do you think we could get away from ——? . . . . CKS
	Shall attempt to get away. . . . MNC
CKNM	—Have (*or, has*) carried away.
	Carried away, or lost, or split——. JQN
	Keep more away. . . . . MHG
CKNP	—Is keeping away.
	AWEIGH. I am aweigh. . . . . . . MNL
	Are you aweigh? . . . . MNQ
CKNQ	AWKWARD-LY-NESS.
	AWNING. . . . . JTB
	AXE-S *or* HATCHETS. . . . . JMQ
CKNR	AXIS.
CKNS	AXLE.
CKNT	AZIMUTH.
CKNV	Azimuth Compass.
	Have you an azimuth compass? GJM
CKNW	—Variation by azimuth.
	————
	B. . . . . WSV
CKPB	BACK-S-ED.
	Ordered back. . . . . CFV
	Back her. . . . . KLP
	Back easy. . . . . KLT
CKPD	—Put-ting back.
CKPF	—Was obliged to put back.
CKPG	—Send back.
CKPH	—Why do you put back?
CKPJ	—Back main-topsail.
CKPL	—Back the——.
	BACKSTAYS. . . . . JQG
CKPM	—Topmast backstays.
	BACKWARD-S. . . . . GFQ
CKPN	BACON.
	Sausages, bacon, hams. . . . . JWK
	BAD. . . . . QKW
CKPQ	—It is very bad.
CKPR	—Is it bad?
CKPS	—Not bad-ly.
CKPT	BAFFLE-S-D-ING.
CKPV	BAG-S.
	Bag. Bale. Sack. Pocket. . . . . VRQ
CKPW	—Coal-bags.
CKQB	—Send bags for.

	BAGS—*cont.*
CKQD	—The ship's bags are sent ashore.
	—Carpet bag. (*See* "CARPET.")
CKQF	—Mail bags.
CKQG	BAGGAGE.
CKQH	BAIL-ED-ABLE.
CKQJ	BAIZE.
CKQL	BAKER.
CKQM	BAKE-S-D-ING.
CKQN	BALANCE-S-D-ING.
	BALE-S. . . . . VRQ
	Bale (*or, manufactured*) goods. NPL
CKQP	BALL-S.
	Ball cartridge-s. . . . . CKL
	—Time ball. (*See* "TIME.")
	BALLAST. . . . . NJC
CKQR	—I am (*or vessel indicated is*) in ballast.
	Ballast (*or, cargo*) has shifted. . NJD
CKQS	—Ballasted with.
CKQT	—Can I obtain ballast at?
	Must take in more ballast. . . . NJH
CKQV	—Ballast can be got at——.
CKQW	—Pig-s of ballast.
	BALLOON-S. . . . . SCQ
CKRB	BALMORAL.
CKRD	BAMBOO-S.
CKRF	BAND-S-ED.
CKRG	BANDAGE-S-D.
CKRH	BANDITTI.
CKRJ	BANISH-ED-MENT.
CKRL	BANK-UP,-S-ED-ING-UP.
	Bank up your fires. . . . . KLW
CKRM	—BANK-S.
CKRN	—BANK OF FRANCE.
CKRP	—BANK OF ENGLAND.
CKRQ	—Bank rate.
	BANK-S. (*See* SHOALS.) . . . . . . LKV
CKRS	—You will be on the bank if you do not alter course.
	You are standing into danger. . . JD
	On the right bank of the river. . GQK
	On the left bank of the river. . . GQL
	Note.—*The right or the left hand bank in descending the stream.*
CKRT	BANKER-S.
CKRV	BANKRUPT-S. . . . . PBW
CKRW	—(*House indicated*) is bankrupt.
	Failures or bankruptcies. . . . . PBV
CKSB	—Agent is bankrupt.
CKSD	—Have any bankruptcies taken place?

Figure 1

[5]

sure there isn't the slightest connection between your code words and their actual meanings.

The other method, which is easier and faster, is to make up groups of letters for your code words. The code book in Figure 1 is an example of this method. These "words" can be made up at random, or they can follow a plan. You might even want to make all your code words pronounceable. That way you could deliver your coded messages verbally. Although our alphabet contains only five or six vowels (a, e, i, o, u, and sometimes y), the twenty-six letters can be arranged to form over 100,000 five-letter pronounceable "words," all different by at least two letters.

Naturally, your code book will be much simpler than the Navy's. I'm sure you can imagine the huge amount of work that went into that one. The makers probably went through an entire dictionary, picking out every word they needed to include in their code book. What a tremendous job! Today, of course, computers would make the job considerably easier.

If you don't want to go through the difficult process of making a code book, you can turn your dictionary into one. Just make sure you and your partner are using exactly the same dictionary!

One way to use the dictionary is to assign each word a five-digit number made up of the number of the page on which the word is found (three digits) and the number of the word on the page (two digits). If the page on which your word appears has fewer than three digits, or if your word appears before the tenth spot on the page, use zeros to make up a five-digit code number. For example, in my dictionary EXER-CISE is the seventh word on page 397, so I would add a zero before 7 and get a code number of 39707.

Here are some other words from *Webster's New Collegiate Dictionary* and their code numbers:

ACADEMY—00611 (eleventh word on page 6)
BABOON—08028 (twenty-eighth word on page 80)
PHANTOM—85207 (seventh word on page 852)
MISTLETOE—73039 (thirty-ninth word on page 730)

If your dictionary has more than 999 pages, as mine does, your code words could easily have six digits. Make sure that you and your friend understand that the last two digits are always the number of the word on the page, while any numbers coming before them refer to the page number.

You might even decide *not* to add zeros to a page number with only one or two digits. In other words, page 3 would be written simply as 3, instead of 03 or 003. By doing that, you will have "words" of various lengths, perhaps confusing an outsider, who might think your code is actually a cipher. This could be an important break for you. Remember, a system of secret writing does not have to baffle your enemies totally. In some cases, it's just as important to confuse them until it's too late for them to act on any information they may get from your message.

The other way to use the dictionary for a code book is just a little more complicated. Start with the page number. Follow this number with an even number between 1 and 9 if your word is in the right-hand column, or an odd number between 1 and 9 if the word is in the left-hand column. Complete your code word with the number of the word in that column.

Let's use PHANTOM as an example. The word appears on page 852 of my dictionary. It's in the left-hand column, and it's the seventh word in that column. Putting it all together, the code word would be 852307. MISTLETOE would now become 730239.

I'm sure you can see that this method of using your dictionary as a code book is not too different from the other method. I've included it to show you that there are variations, however slight, of most of the basic methods of sending secret messages. Don't be afraid to add to the basics if a new system will suit your needs better than the one I've explained.

You probably recognize one of the disadvantages of using codes. You must have a code book. If it is bulky, it will be difficult to carry around with you. It can be lost, stolen, or destroyed. For these reasons, a code book is usually used in permanent espionage locations rather than by agents constantly on the move. On warships, code books always have lead covers. If a ship is captured, the code book is quickly thrown overboard. Because of the lead covers, the book falls to the bottom of the sea.

On the other hand, there are some advantages to using a code system. Generally, it is easier to work with codes than with ciphers. Encoding and decoding can be done more quickly than enciphering and deciphering. Also, a code system is usually more secure than a cipher system. If you break a cipher message, you probably will be able to figure out the system and then easily break other messages that use the same one. This isn't necessarily the case with code systems. Look again at the Navy code, and you'll see there is really no connection between one word and any other word on the page.

You must be very careful when you transmit a coded message, because a mistake may very well result in another message. Using the Navy code, you can see that CKQL means BAKER. However, CKQG means BAGGAGE, and CKQP means BALL. One mistake and your message will be quite different, won't it? However, in a cipher message, since you have a one-to-one correspondence between your plaintext and your secret message, a mistake or two may not be disastrous, because you should be able to detect the error from the way the word is used in the message.

If you were a *cryptographer*, whose business is codes and secret writing, you might carry your code system a step further. After you had encoded your message you might encipher it, using one of the systems explained later in this book. Such a message is said to be *superenciphered*. What a challenge a superenciphered message would present to the person trying to crack it!

In addition to the military, there have been other groups of people in this country who have developed their own codes. One of these groups is the hoboes, the men and women of the 1920s and 1930s who were out of work. They crisscrossed the country in search of jobs and better living conditions. But because life was difficult all over the country during the Depression, many hoboes traveled aimlessly.

In their travels, the hoboes developed a system of picture codes to help other hoboes who happened to pass through the same towns and neighborhoods. Some of their signs warned other hoboes about unfriendly policemen or vicious dogs. Others gave the wanderers encouragement or good tips. Figure 2 shows some of the signs that many hoboes would recognize immediately.

Figure 2

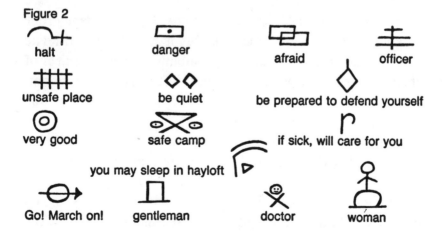

halt

danger

afraid

officer

unsafe place

be quiet

be prepared to defend yourself

very good

safe camp

if sick, will care for you

you may sleep in hayloft

Go! March on!

gentleman

doctor

woman

Suppose you wanted to give hoboes who passed through your neighborhood some help. Can you think of things to warn them against? How about grouchy storekeepers or dangerous places to hide out? What about some of the pleasant aspects of your neighborhood that hoboes would like to know about? You may have to come up with some new symbols that express your neighborhood. Using the ones in Figure 2 as a guide, draw the new symbols in your notebook. Then take a walk through your neighborhood to see if there's anything you've forgotten to say about it. I think you'll be surprised to find that you need to come up with even more symbols.

It might also be fun to think of hobo signs that apply to your school. What would you want to tell a new student about your school (besides the lunch!)? Talk it over with your friends. I'm sure you could come up with a great list.

Another group of Americans who had their own code system was the cowboys, those rugged men who raised cattle. There was a difference, however, between the hobo code and the cowboy brand. The brand was a sign of possession. It told everyone that someone owned a steer. Figure 3 shows you the branding alphabet.

Of course, people had to be able to read the brands in order to know who owned the cattle. But it wasn't difficult. The cowboys made their brands by combining different parts of their alphabet in a particular order: left to right, top to bottom, outside to inside. For example, a K inside a circle was the Circle K, not the K Circle.

How about trying to decode some of the brands in Figure 4? Remember the rules and consult the chart in Figure 3 for help.

Would you like to come up with a brand of your own? You could use it to mark some of your possessions. If none of the

Letters, Numbers and Variations

ℳ	Running W
W	Long W
Ʀ	Tumbling right R
Ʀ	Tumbling left R
Я	Reverse R
Ʀ	Crazy R
Я	Crazy reverse R
⊏	Lazy left down R
⊏	Lazy left up R
⊐	Lazy right down R
⊐	Lazy right up R
⌐7	Rocking 7
7	Swinging 7
7̄	Flying 7
7	Walking 7
7	Dragging 7
Ỿ	Hooked Y
Y	Bradded Y
Ỿ	Barbed Y
X	Forked Y
Y⅄	Y up Y down
KM	KM connected
KKK	Triple K

Geometric Symbols

✳	Triple K connected
—	Bar
=	Double bar
⌒	Broken bar
—	Rail
=	Double rail
≡	Stripes
/	Slash
\	Reverse slash
⟋	Broken slash
⟍	Broken reverse slash
⌒	Quarter circle
⌒	Half circle
◯	Circle
◎	Double circle
⊓	Half box
□	Box
⌐	Bench
△	Triangle
⟨	Half diamond
◇	Diamond
⋈	Diamond and a half
⌢	Rafter

Pictorial Symbols

◅	Arrow
⅃	Broken arrow
Ψ	Bow and arrow
⊔	Rocking chair
$	Dollar sign
⚓	Anchor
♡	Broken heart
♡	Flying heart
⌐o	Hay hook
o⊤	Key
▦	Tumbling ladder
☼	Spur
⌂	Stirrup
☋	Sunrise
⋒	Horse track
⋎	Bull head
⌂	Hat
Ψ	Turkey track

Open A ⋀

Goose egg ◯

Dot •

Figure 3

Figure 4

[11]

symbols in Figure 3 works for you, why not design some additions to the branding alphabet? Perhaps you'll want symbols that are more modern or a little zany. Your brand certainly doesn't have to be serious. J. H. Barwise, a rancher of the last century, used a funny brand that was equivalent to his last name: $\overline{YY}$. If you read his brand according to the rules (top to bottom), you have Bar Y's! Get it?

You could also use the idea behind brands to create symbols for people and places in your community. Then you could include those symbols in your code book and in your secret messages. Any book on maps or mapmaking will give you ideas for symbols. Figures 5 and 6 show examples of symbols used on maps.

In the past fifteen years or so, road signs have undergone a change. More and more, pictures replace words on signs in big cities or near airports or large public places. Figure 7 shows some common picture signs that you might come across while traveling.

Figure 5

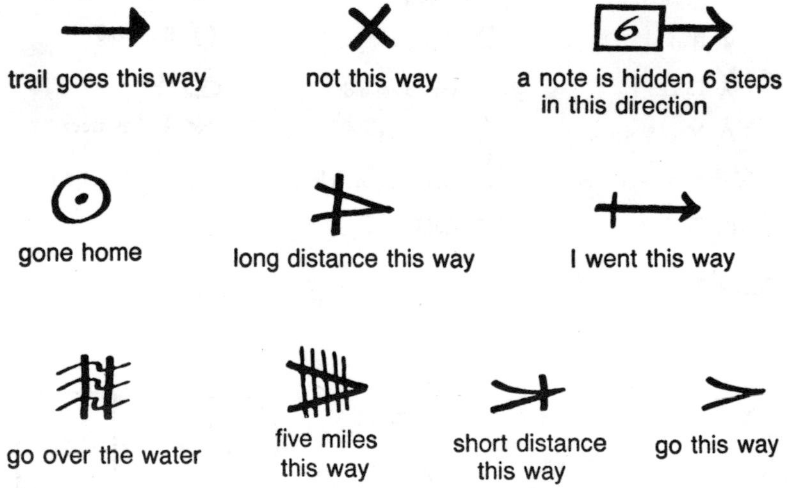

trail goes this way

not this way

a note is hidden 6 steps in this direction

gone home

long distance this way

I went this way

go over the water

five miles this way

short distance this way

go this way

[12]

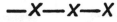

bridge   telephone or
          telegraph wires   barbed wire fence

schoolhouse   hospital   church   camp

airplane
landing field   mine or quarry   railroad track   factory

Figure 6

Figure 7

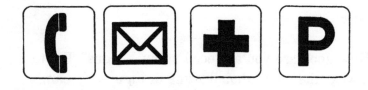

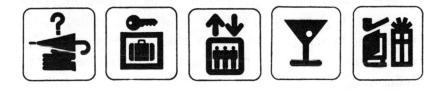

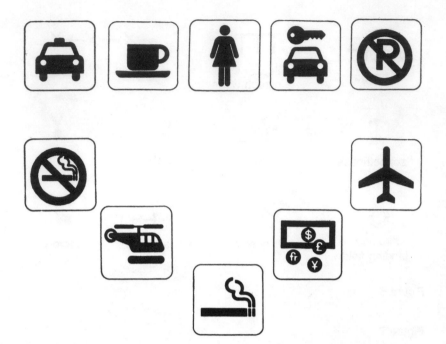

Figure 8

How good are you at decoding such signs? Try to figure out what the international signs in Figure 8 mean.

Another possibility for your code book is a picture language. When people began to communicate by writing, they did so with pictures. These pictures, called *pictographs*, were used by many of the Indian tribes in this country. Figure 9 shows some of the pictographs that were used by the Indians.

There are some limitations to pictographs. How would you use a picture to communicate an abstract idea or feeling? What picture would communicate love or sadness or joy? Also, there is no way to indicate verb tense. For example, we don't know if the story shown in Figure 10 is about what happened or what is going to happen. Try to decode this story, reading from left to right. Check over the signs in

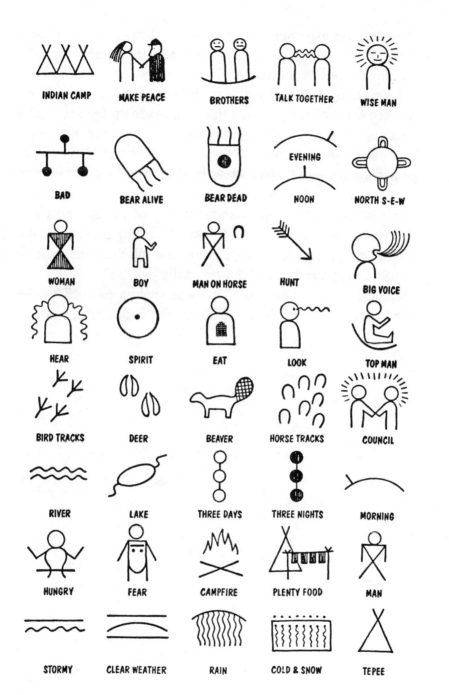

Figure 9

[15]

Figure 9 and use your imagination for those signs you don't know. Remember that pictographs indicate number by adding small lines to a picture.

How about writing a pictograph message to a friend? You can use some of the symbols that you made up for your hobo language, but you will probably have to add some new ones.

If you take the time to follow up on some of these ideas, your code book will soon grow in size. It will contain many useful symbols that you can include in your secret messages. Don't be afraid to make changes in any of the symbols you find in this book or in other books. And remember to make your symbols simple enough to get the job done, but not so simple that your system can be easily cracked.

Some codes are used exclusively as spoken codes. These—Pig Latin, Opish, and Turkey Irish—are impractical to work

Figure 10

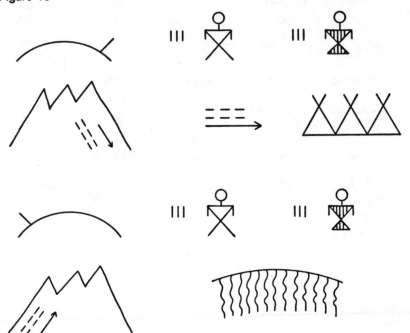

with on paper, but sound amazing when spoken swiftly and accurately. To get these codes to sound great, you'll have to practice them as you would any foreign language.

The most widely known of these codes is *Pig Latin*. Don't be put off by the name. It has nothing to do with pigs *or* Latin. There are only two steps to putting a message into Pig Latin. First, if your word begins with a vowel, add WAY to the word. For example, END becomes ENDWAY. Some other translations: ANT—ANTWAY, EVEN—EVENWAY, UNITED—UNITEDWAY. Second, for words that start with consonants, move the first letter to the end of the word, then add AY. If the consonant sound is made up of two letters, move both letters to the end of the word. So, CODE becomes ODECAY, BOOK becomes OOKBAY. Some others: HAT—ATHAY, TABLE—ABLETAY, WORLD—ORLDWAY. And THE becomes ETHAY.

Looks easy to decode, doesn't it? That's because these are only a few isolated printed examples. However, if you put together all the words of a message and speak them rapidly, the results will be puzzling, and somewhat amusing. Try saying this sentence out loud: ETHAY OOKBAY ELLFAY ONWAY ISHAY EADHAY. Translation: THE BOOK FELL ON HIS HEAD. The key is to know the rules well enough so that you can use them without really thinking.

Let's try some more. See if you can say, then translate, these Pig Latin sentences into English:

1. AMPAY ATEWAY WOTAY AWRAY ISHFAY ODAYTAY.
2. ANCAY IGSPAY EALLYRAY EAKSPAY ATINLAY?
3. ETHAY EDRAY OXSAY AYPLAY ATWAY ENWAYFAY ARKPAY.

Now try writing the following sentences in Pig Latin. Then say them out loud, because that's what Pig Latin is all about.

1. LISTENING TO RECORDS IS GREAT FUN.
2. I LIKE TO BIKE IN THE SUMMER.
3. MY BLACK DOG IS NAMED ED.

Opish is another spoken code language. All you do is add OP *after each consonant.* So, CAR becomes COPAROP, HAT becomes HOPATOP. Try translating these words:

1. BOPOOKOP
2. DOPROPIVOPE
3. LOPAWOPNOP

Try translating these sentences into Opish and then saying them out loud:

1. HE WENT SWIMMING IN THE POND.
2. MEET ME AT THE END OF THE TUNNEL AT NOON.
3. THE CONCERT WILL BE HELD IN THE PARK.

Turkey Irish is similar to Opish except that in this spoken code you will add AB *before every vowel.* FENCE becomes FABENCABE, CART becomes CABART. You may run into trouble with words that have vowels repeated, like TREE, or with words that have different vowels together, like BEACH. The best thing to do with words like these is to work with the first vowel. In other words, you would say TREE as TRABEE, and BEACH as BABEACH.

See what you can do with these Turkey Irish sentences:

1. HABE SABAT ABON THABE RABED
   BABENCH.
2. THABE GABIRL LABOST ABALL HABER
   HABAIR.
3. MABY SABOUP WABAS CABOLD.

Put these sentences into Turkey Irish:

1. THE CAT CRIED AT THE BACK DOOR.
2. MY SISTER IS A LAWYER AND BASEBALL
   FAN.
3. SUMMERTIME IS REALLY A TIME FOR FUN.

These spoken codes can come in handy, especially if your parents—like mine—speak a second language when they don't want anyone to know what they're talking about. You can use these codes as your own secret language.

Answers to Chapter 1

Translation of Figure 4, page 11:

1. Diamond J
2. Rafter P
3. Double Rail Triangle
4. Circle T
5. Box Dot

Translation of Figure 7, page 13:

Top row, left to right:
Telephone, Mail, First Aid, Parking
Middle row, left to right:
Lost and Found, Baggage Lockers, Elevator,
Cocktail Lounge, Gift Shop
Bottom row, left to right:
Men's Room, Bus, Restaurant, Luggage Claim

Translation of Figure 8, page 14:

Top row, left to right:
Taxi, Coffee Shop, Ladies' Room, Lock Your Car,
No Parking
Bottom row, left to right:
No Smoking, Helicopter, Smoking Permitted,
Currency Exchange, Airport

Translation of Figure 10, page 16:

At sunset, three men and three women came down from
the mountains and entered camp. In the morning, three
men and three women climbed back up the mountain while
it rained.

Translations of Pig Latin, page 17:

1. Pam ate two raw fish today.
2. Can pigs really speak Latin?
3. The Red Sox play at Fenway Park.

Translations into Pig Latin, page 18:

1. ISTENINGLAY OTAY ECORDSRAY ISWAY
   EATGRAY UNFAY.
2. IWAY IKELAY OTAY IKEBAY INWAY ETHAY
   UMMERSAY.
3. YMAY ACKBLAY OGDAY ISWAY AMEDNAY
   EDWAY.

Translations of Opish, page 18:

1. book
2. drive
3. lawn

Translations into Opish, page 18:

1. HOPE WOPENOPTOP SOPWOPIMOPMOPINOPGOP
   INOP TOPHOPE POPONOPDOP.
2. MOPEETOP MOPE ATOP TOPHOPE ENOPDOP OFOP
   TOPHOPE TOPUNOPNOPELOP ATOP NOPOONOP.
3. TOPHOPE COPONOPCOPEROPTOP WOPILOPLOP
   BOPE HOPELOPDOP INOP TOPHOPE
   POPAROPKOP.

Translations of Turkey Irish, page 19:

1. He sat on the red bench.
2. The girl lost all her hair.
3. My soup was cold.

[21]

Translations into Turkey Irish, page 19:

1. THABE CABAT CRABIED ABAT THABE BABACK
   DABOOR.
2. MABY SABISTABER ABIS ABA LABAWABYER
   ABAND BABASABEBABALL FABAN.
3. SABUMMABERTABIMABE ABIS RABEALLABY ABA
   TABIMABE FABOR FABUN.

Chapter 2

Only the Trained Eye:

Basic Concealment Tactics

Can you remember a time when you hid something from someone? Maybe it was something you didn't want your parents or your nosy little brother to find. Maybe you had to hide something from a teacher. If you did a good job, you might have a talent for working with secret messages, because an important part of sending a secret message is the ability to conceal it from your enemy.

Some of the methods of concealment that were used by the ancient Greeks were downright cruel and painful. When Histiaeus, a Greek ambassador to Persia, wanted to send secret political and military information to people in Greece, he would find a slave who complained about bad eyesight and use him as a messenger. Telling the slave that he could cure his vision problem, Histiaeus shaved the slave's head. Then, painfully, he branded his message on the slave's skull! Once the hair grew back on the slave's head, Histiaeus sent him to Greece, saying that his eyesight would be cured when his head was shaved there. The unsuspecting slave knew nothing about the message on his skull.

[23]

Other Greeks were even more cruel in the treatment of their slaves for political or military reasons. Some drugged their slaves and branded their backs with secret messages. After the effects of the drugs had worn off, they told their slaves that when they reached their destination, a healing ointment would be applied to their backs.

The Greeks also had more humane methods of concealment. One involved writing their messages on a tablet of wood, then covering the tablet with a layer of wax. On the wax they wrote their fake message. When the tablet was exposed to heat, the wax melted and the real message was revealed.

Tacitus, a famous Roman historian, described in his writings a few interesting methods of concealment. One technique was wrapping a soldier's wounds with a bandage that contained a secret message. Another was sewing a letter into the sole of a person's shoe. Perhaps the most clever technique was writing a message on a thin sheet of lead, then rolling the metal into an earring.

While these methods of hiding a secret message are too cruel or too intricate for us, they do show us the lengths to which some people went in order to conceal their messages. Perhaps they will encourage you to come up with some exciting concealment techniques of your own. Make sure your methods work, however, or you may wind up like the man who believed that if words were spoken into a tube sealed at one end, then quickly corked at the other end, the sound would remain in the tube until it was uncorked!

Let's look at some concealment techniques that are more practical. Perhaps the easiest method of concealment is the *space code*. All you have to do is break up the words in your message into meaningless-looking units. Here's an example. If I wanted to say SEND ME THE FILM SOON, I could write SE NDM ET HEFI LMSO ON. Or I could write SEN

DME TH EFI LMS OON. The problem with this system is that your partner will have to do little hunting to find your message.

For practice, use the space code to encode the following messages in your notebook. Try to come up with a couple of variations for each message.

1. YOU MUST MEET THE TRAIN AT NOON WITHOUT FAIL.
2. CARGO SHOULD ARRIVE BEFORE NIGHTFALL.
3. CONTACT THIS NUMBER IF THERE ARE PROBLEMS.

If you want to send a short message, you might try the *playing card code*. All you do is write your message lightly in pencil on the edge of a deck of playing cards. Shuffle the cards and give them to your partner. When your partner arranges the cards in an order that was agreed upon in advance, he or she will get your message.

The *puncture cipher* is an interesting method of sending a secret message. First of all, get a newspaper or magazine and find an article that you want to use for your message. With a pin, make a slight puncture over each letter of your message. Of course, you have to puncture your letters in the order in which they appear in your message, because your partner will be copying them down and then trying to find the words they form.

The puncture cipher originated in the Middle Ages, but it became very popular in England in the seventeenth and eighteenth centuries. At that time it cost more money to send a letter than it did to send a newspaper, so people would use the puncture cipher to send their letters in newspapers! Following is one example of a puncture cipher message:

The Eastern Seaboard's first major storm of the winter spread ice and snow Tuesday from Mississippi to Maine, giving thousands of schoolchildren a holiday.

Accumulations were more than a foot deep in places. Almost a foot of snow already was on the ground in Utica, N.Y., by early afternoon, with eight inches in Rochester, N.Y., and in northern Ohio. Parts of Maine were expected to get well over eighteen inches of new snow by the time the storm moved out to sea late Wednesday morning.

A *null cipher* uses a fixed letter of each word in a fake message to communicate its real meaning. There are two ways to use the null cipher. One is to write a legitimate-sounding message and work the proper letters into it. Here is an example using the first letter of each word to convey the message: SOME TENTS OPEN PRETTY EASILY AND RE-QUIRE LITTLE YANKING. As you can imagine, this method is very difficult and takes a lot of time. The other way, which is much easier, is to use words that have absolutely no meaning in relation to each other. This could baffle your enemy even more, because he or she might be looking for some connection between the words.

Following are examples of the second method. In each one, note the last letter of every word to find my secret message.

1. AMMONIA DANGER BELIEVE MINI PAN BREAD SEA DOWN SAILING EYE MEMBER.
2. SIP SELL SEE SEA SASS SAME SHEER SIZE SHARP SOLO SCAR SHEET.
3. RIDER MOVE LET YOU MINISTER ACORN BENT SILO PLANTED SEA TODAY.
4. RAM LEDGE DONATE TREAT HYENA PET GRIP AREA POOR HACK.
5. PACIFIC MIMOSA HERBAL BASEBALL TEST

TO EXPLOSION HOUDINI DANCING
UNCOUTH LIMIT.

Try your hand at encoding the following four messages.
Feel free to flip through the dictionary until you come up with
words that end in the letters you need.

1. BEWARE OF DANGERS.
2. MEETING SET FOR FRIDAY.
3. ESCAPE TO COAST.
4. HIDE IN BUSHES.

Here is a system of concealment that requires working
with your hands. You'll need a piece of soft wood (poplar or
pine will work well) and a hobby knife with a sharp point. An
art teacher in your school might lend you one and might even
help you use it. Remember, it has a very sharp point, and you
should use it without adult supervision only if you are very
experienced. And, regardless of your experience, be careful.

With the knife, cut your message into the wood. Don't
carve out the letters. Just cut them into the wood about a
quarter of an inch deep. Make sure they are neat. After
you've made the cuts, hammer the letters or clamp the wood
in a vise until the letters are no longer visible. How can you
make the letters reappear? Dampen the wood!

Another concealment technique is to make, say, every
third word in a fake sentence part of a real message. Of
course, you and your partner would have to agree to this in
advance. Using this technique, find the real message in these
notes:

1. WHEN YOU FOLLOW ONLY THE SAFE AND
   SENSIBLE ROUTE YOU'RE UNLIKELY TO
   FIND ANY FREEDOM FROM BOREDOM.

2. THE SAME MAN YOU SAW WILL WANT TO
MEET LATER WITH YOU BUT NOT AT THE
SWANEE RIVER DOWN SOUTH.

Try writing a few messages like these in your notebook. You might want to vary the technique by using every second or fourth word for your secret message.

A more difficult method of concealing a secret message is with a *grille*, a piece of paper with holes or windows cut out of it. To make a grille, you're going to need a few 3″ by 5″ file cards, some tracing paper, a ruler, the hobby knife, and a pen or pencil.

First, trace the form in Figure 11 on your paper. Then place the paper over a file card and cut along the window lines through both the paper and the card. Again, be very careful with the hobby knife, and, if you haven't used it a lot, get help from somebody who has. Also, be sure to place a

Figure 11

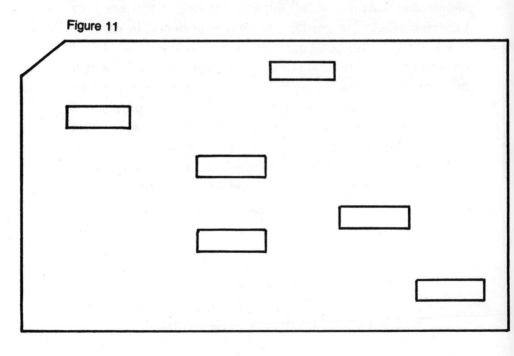

piece of cardboard under your work so you do not cut into your table or desk.

Your grille must look exactly like the one in Figure 11. If your windows are out of place, the grille will not work. Once your grille has been cut out, you can encode your message.

For our exercise, let's use the following message: CALL ME TOMORROW NIGHT AT SEVEN AT THE USUAL NUMBER. I WILL BE READY TO GIVE YOU THE DE- TAILS YOU WILL NEED FOR WORK. The message con- tains twenty-four words that will fit exactly into the grille. However, as you will see later, longer and shorter messages can also be handled easily.

Place the grille over another file card so that the cut-off corner is on top at the left. Now, going from top to bottom, left to right, write each of the first six words of the message in the windows, one per window. When you lift the grille, your file card should look like the one in Figure 12.

Figure 12

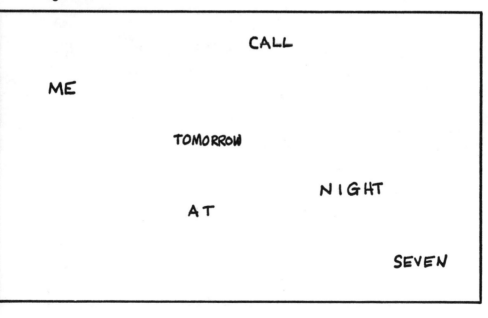

Next, flip the grille over so that the cut-off corner is on the lower left-hand side. Write in the next six words the same way you wrote in the first six. Your file card should now look like the one in Figure 13.

Flip the grille again, this time so that the cut-off corner is on the lower right-hand side. Write in the next six words. Then turn the grille so that the cut-off corner is on the upper right-hand side, and write in the last six words of the message. When you lift the grille after the fourth flip, your file card will look like the one in Figure 14.

Do not send this file card to your partner. Because of the geometric arrangement of the words, it would be a dead giveaway to the wrong person. Instead, write out the words on another piece of paper and send *that* to your partner. Your written message should look like one long nonsense sentence: BE DETAILS CALL AT ME THE READY YOU TO TOMORROW WILL USUAL NEED NUMBER GIVE

Figure 13

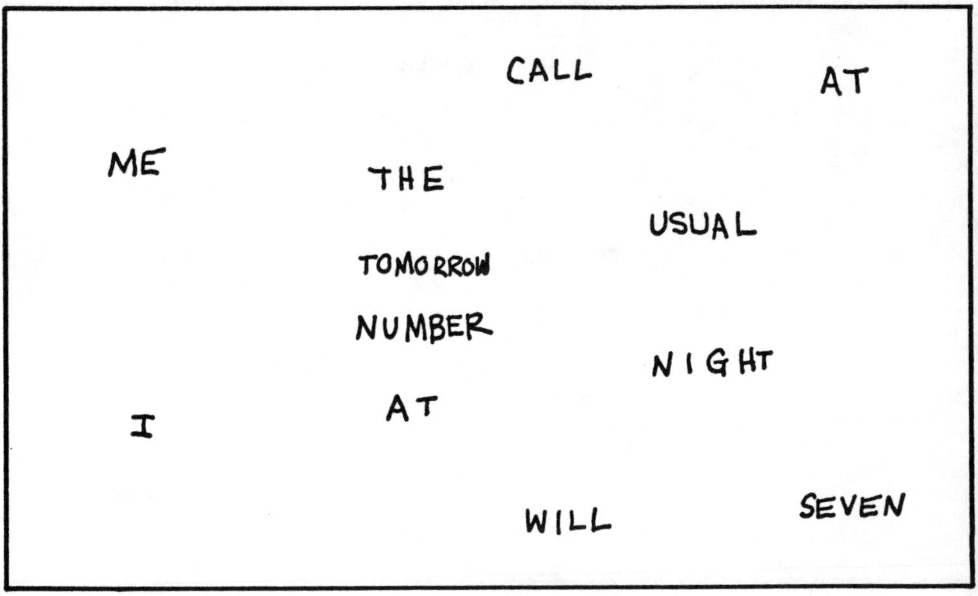

CALL   AT

ME   THE

USUAL

TOMORROW

NUMBER

NIGHT

I   AT

WILL   SEVEN

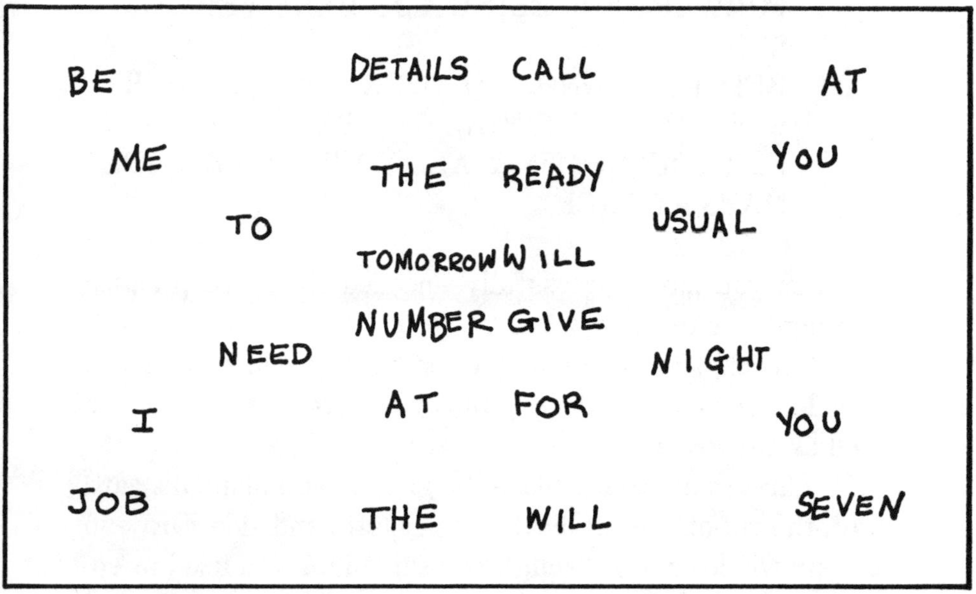

Figure 14

NIGHT I AT FOR YOU JOB THE WILL SEVEN.

If your message is longer than twenty-four words, handle twenty-four words at a time on a separate file card. Simply follow the steps I've just shown you. If your message is shorter than twenty-four words, fill in the remaining windows with *nulls*. A null is a meaningless word or letter inserted in a message to fill an empty space.

How about a little practice? Using the grille in Figure 11, encode these three messages:

1. YOUR COVER IS BLOWN. IT IS IMPORTANT THAT YOU CONTACT ME AT THIS OFFICE AS SOON AS YOU KNOW YOU ARE NOT BEING FOLLOWED.
2. CONGRATULATIONS ON A GOOD JOB. YOUR SHIPMENT ARRIVED EARLY TODAY IN EXCELLENT SHAPE. WELL DONE. I LOOK

FORWARD TO SEEING YOU HERE VERY
SOON.
3. REPORT AT ONCE TO YOUR AREA LEADER.
SHE WILL HAVE NEW ESCAPE ROUTE MAPS
FOR YOU. DESTROY ALL YOUR OLD ESCAPE
MAPS AT ONCE.

When you have successfully encoded the three practice
messages, you will be set to try your hand at decoding. It's
a little tricky, but you shouldn't have any real trouble. To
decode, you will need the supplies you have already used, as
well as the grille.

The first thing to do is place the grille over a blank file card
with the cut-off corner on the upper left-hand side. Draw in
the six windows. Go through the same flips you used in encoding, drawing in six windows with each flip. Once you've
flipped the grille four times, your file card should look like the
one in Figure 15.

Figure 15

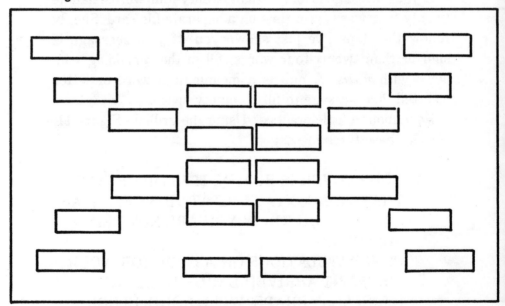

Next, going from top to bottom, left to right, write one word of the original secret message in each of the windows. This must be done *in the order in which the words appear.* Start with the first six words of the message on page 30, which are BE DETAILS CALL AT ME THE. When you have finished, your windows will be filled in like those in Figure 16.

Now take your grille and place it over the filled-in card, with the cut-off corner on the upper left-hand side. You will see the first six words of the message. Then flip the grille three times. Each time you do, you'll see six new words of the original message.

Try it. Here are three messages for you to decode.

1. BY TO PURPLE FAMOUS WAS CIPHER
   AMERICANS BREAK IN THE MANY MACHINE
   JAPANESE THAT WORLD NAME WAS OF
   SECRET WAR MESSAGES TWO USED A.
2. AND GERMANS ANOTHER THE IMPORTANT

Figure 16

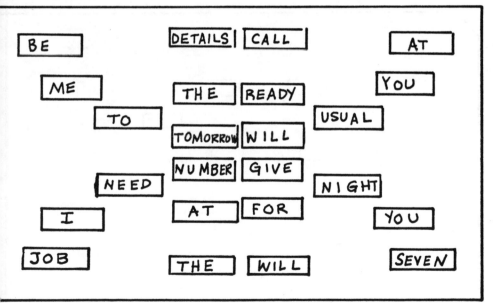

BRITISH IT IN WAS CIPHER THE ARMY
SECOND WAS USED MACHINE CALLED USED
WORLD AGAINST WAR THE ENIGMA BY.
3. TWO AND THE THE MAN CIPHER RISKED
PARTS HIS WHO PAST MACHINES THE
DURING LIFE INVENTED WORLD ONE
ENEMY SMUGGLING LINES BLUEPRINTS
WAR OF.

Another way to use a grille is to have it reveal a message hidden in a group of readable words. For example, you could write an innocent-looking letter to a friend who, on placing over the letter a grille that the two of you have agreed to use, would find your message.

Let's say that you and your friend have agreed to write notes to each other on index cards and that you have decided to use the grille in Figure 17.

Figure 17

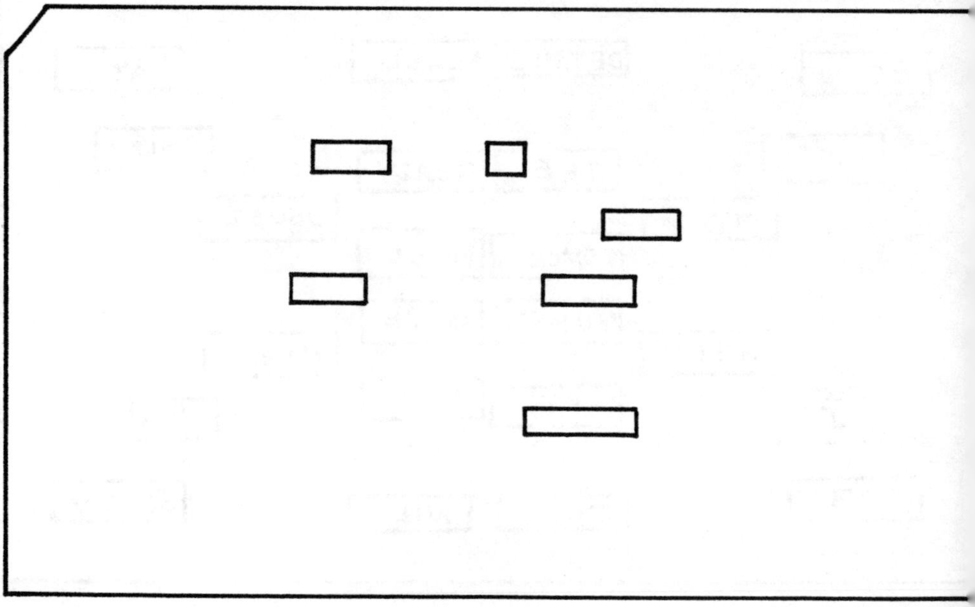

After making the grille (just as you did the one in Figure 11), place it over the following note.

WAIT UNTIL YOU HEAR WHAT HAPPENED TO ME. MY
MOM WENT TO MEET DAD AT THE STORE. I DIDN'T
KNOW WHEN THEY WERE COMING BACK, BUT SHE
LOCKED THE DOOR ON ME! AFTER I TRIED THE
WINDOWS, I KNEW I WAS STUCK. I THOUGHT I'D
STARVE IF I DIDN'T EAT SUPPER SOON. LUCKY
FOR ME, THEY FINALLY RESCUED ME.

What is your secret message? Of course, if you had actually written this, you would have written the secret message first, constructing the letter around it. And you would have been very careful to write a letter that made sense. After all, if you use words that don't seem to belong in your letter, an outsider who sees it will know that something is up.

Needless to say, you do not have to send your letters on index cards. You can use any stationery you like—provided that you and your friend use identical grilles.

The *dot cipher* is still another system of concealment. It could also be called the *line cipher* or the *zigzag cipher.* You'll see why.

To begin with, you will need a *key*, an alphabet arranged in any order you and your partner have agreed to. For our key, let's use the alphabet in its normal order. Print it across the top of a piece of paper, making sure your letters are neat and evenly spaced. If you have a typewriter, you should use it.

To write a message, line up another piece of paper under the key. It's important that you mark the position of the paper under the key so that it stays in place while you're writing. Now, write the message COME AT NOON TO THE OLD CHURCH. First, put a dot under the C. Next, move your pencil down a little bit and put a dot under the O. Move down a little more and put a dot under the M. Get the idea? Your completed message should look like the one shown in Figure 18.

Figure 18

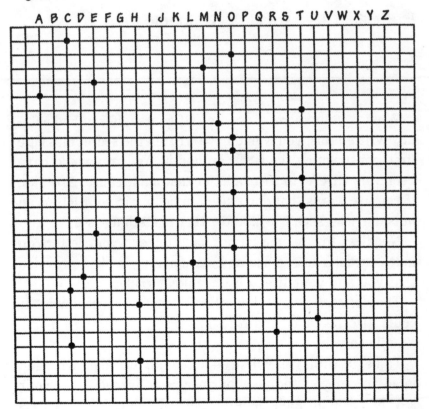

If you want to make a line cipher, simply connect *every two dots* with a straight line. You will then get a cipher like the one in Figure 19.

You must be very careful that your lines are drawn perfectly, because your partner is going to line up your paper under his or her key. If your lines are just a little too long or a little too short, the message will be more difficult to read.

If you connected *all the dots in order*, you would have a zigzag cipher, and it would look like the cipher shown in Figure 20.

To decipher a zigzag cipher, simply follow the line from the top of the page to the point at which it changes direction by

Figure 19

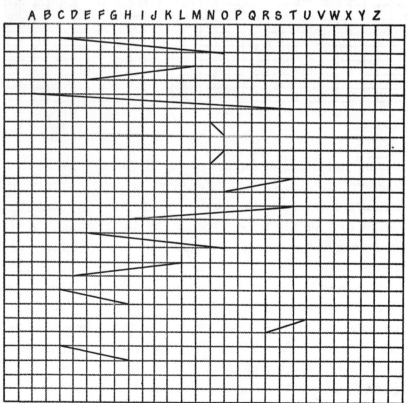

A B C D E F G H I J K L M N O P Q R S T U V W X Y Z

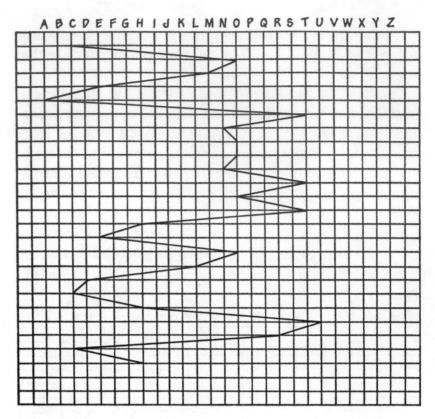

Figure 20

moving right, left, or farther down. The letters are located wherever the line changes direction. Again, be sure your lines are drawn accurately.

How can you use the dot cipher and its variations? Well, the easiest way is to send your friend the piece of paper with the dots or lines on it. However, you could also put the dots on a page of a newspaper or magazine that you and your partner have preselected. Once you've gotten the paper or magazine to your partner, he or she will know exactly which page to turn to. You could even draw the dots or lines with invisible ink (see Appendix 3).

Time for some practice. Use the key in Figure 18 to enci-

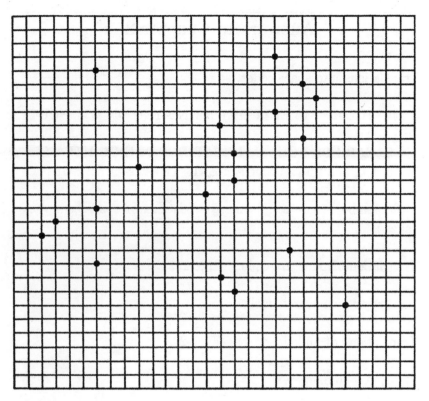

Figure 21

pher this message: BE CAREFUL OF DOTS AND LINES. After you've enciphered this message, try to decipher the bunch of dots shown in Figure 21. Again, use the key in Figure 18.

Translations into space codes, page 25:

1. YOUMU STMEETT HET RAIN ATNO ON WIT HOUTF AIL.
2. CARG OS HOUL DARR IVE BEF ORENIG HTFA LL.
3. CONTA CTTHI SNUMB ERIF THER EAREP ROB LEMS.

(Remember, there can be many variations of space code messages.)

Translation of puncture cipher, page 26:

Try to hide secrets well.

Translations of null cipher, pages 26–27:

1. Are in danger.
2. Please report.
3. Return today.
4. Meet at park.
5. Call tonight.

Translations of "every-third-word" code, pages 27–28:

1. Follow safe route to freedom.
2. Man will meet you at river.

Translation into grille code, pages 31–32:

1. THIS KNOW YOUR IMPORTANT COVER THAT OFFICE YOU AS IS ARE YOU NOT CONTACT SOON BLOWN ME IT BEING AS FOLLOWED YOU AT IS.
2. SHAPE TO CONGRATULATIONS SHIPMENT ON

ARRIVED WELL SEEING DONE A YOU EARLY
HERE TODAY I GOOD IN JOB VERY LOOK SOON
FORWARD EXCELLENT YOUR.
3. ROUTE YOUR REPORT LEADER AT SHE MAPS OLD
FOR ONCE ESCAPE WILL MAPS HAVE YOU TO
NEW YOUR AT DESTROY ONCE ALL ESCAPE
AREA.

Translations of grille code, pages 33–34:

1. Purple was the name of a famous cipher machine that
   was used by Americans in World War Two to break
   many Japanese secret messages.
2. Another important cipher machine used by the British
   Army was called Enigma, and it was used against the
   Germans in the Second World War.
3. The man who invented one of the cipher machines during
   World War Two risked his life smuggling blueprints and
   parts past the enemy lines.

Translation of grille code, page 35:

Meet at back door after supper.

Translation of dot cipher, page 39:

Return to home base now.

Chapter 3
Wheels and Slides:
Substitution Ciphers

The substitution cipher—in which one symbol is substituted for another—was first used at least two thousand years ago. Julius Caesar invented a simple system that bears his name: the *Caesar cipher*. The Caesar cipher shifts the alphabet *forward* three places to create a new alphabet for sending secret messages. It looks like this next to the alphabet:

A B C D E F G H I J K L M N O P Q R S T U V W X Y Z

X Y Z A B C D E F G H I J K L M N O P Q R S T U V W

So if you wanted to send the message BEWARE OF TREACHERY, you would write YBTXOB LC QOBX-ZEBOV. It's that simple. How about a little practice? In your notebook, try deciphering these messages, using the Caesar cipher:

1. QEB ZXBPXO ZFMEBO FP SBOV LIA.
2. TLOHFKD TFQE ZFMEBOP QXHBP MOXZQFZB.

3. VLR ZXK EFAB PBZOBQP TFQE ZFMEBOP.

A variation of the Caesar cipher is the *St. Cyr cipher*, named after the French national military academy where it was taught in the 1880s. To make a St. Cyr cipher slide, you will need paper, felt-tip markers, and a hobby knife.

First, print the alphabet across a sheet of paper. This alphabet is called the *stator*. Then cut two slits (carefully) below the alphabet, on either side of it. Now, on a strip of paper narrow enough to slip through the slits and twice as long as the stator (you can simply put two strips together), print out the alphabet twice. Make sure that the spacing is the same as it is on the stator. Your slide can now be moved in either direction to select letters that you would like to substitute for the alphabet. When completed, your St. Cyr cipher slide should look like the one shown in Figure 22.

Figure 22

The alphabets on the slide need not be written in order, as I have written them in my example. If you wish, you may use random alphabets, that is, alphabets with scrambled letters. That way, if someone intercepted your message, it would be more difficult for that person to break your cipher.

As you have seen, both the Caesar cipher and the St. Cyr cipher use the letters of the alphabet in the plaintext as well as in the enciphered message. But this does not have to be true of all substitution ciphers. You can substitute anything you can think of for the letters of the alphabet, and you can make your system as easy or as difficult as you want it to be.

Another easy substitution cipher system uses the numbers 1 through 26 instead of the letters of the alphabet. There are, of course, many variations of this system. Here are five variations:

1. reversed numbers (26–1)
2. odd numbers
3. even numbers
4. odd numbers reversed
5. even numbers reversed

To send the message CALL AT THE HOTEL AT TWO, using the 1–26 system, you would write the following: 3-1-12-12 1-20 20-8-5 8-15-20-5-12 1-20 20-23-15. Can you think of other variations of this system? Make a list of them in your notebook.

Before we go on to other systems, let's have another practice session. Using variation 3 from above, decipher this message: 50-30-42 26-2-50 12-18-28-8 40-16-18-38 38-50-38-40-10-26 26-30-36-10 8-18-12-12-18-6-42-24-40 40-16-2-28 40-16-10 30-40-16-10-36 30-28-10.

Now decipher this, using variation 5: 46-24 26-24-14 50-44 52 30-36-14-14-44-18-50-12-40.

Keep in mind that you can use the St. Cyr cipher slide with any variation of the Caesar cipher. All you have to do is put your numbers on the slide. Try making another St. Cyr cipher slide with numbers.

Another substitution system was used by the American writer Edgar Allan Poe (1809–1849) in one of his stories. Poe is known for his weird and sinister short stories and poems, but he was also very interested in codes and ciphers. In "The

Gold Bug," Legrand, the main character, must unravel the message shown in Figure 23.

53‡‡†305))6*;4826)4‡.)4‡);806*;48†8¶60))
85;;]8*;:‡*8†83(88)5*†;46(;88*96*?;8)*‡(;485);
5*†2:*‡(;4956*2(5*—4)8¶8*;4069285);)6†8)
4‡‡;1(‡9;48081;8:8‡1;48†85;4)485†528806*81(
‡9;48;(88;4(‡?34;48)4‡;161;:188;‡?;

Figure 23

After applying some elementary rules of codebreaking (which we will cover in Chapter 5), Legrand is able to come up with the letters shown in Figure 24.

5 represents a
† represents d
8 represents e
3 represents g
4 represents h
6 represents i
* represents n
‡ represents o
(represents r
; represents t

Figure 24

Using Legrand's clues, try to crack this mystery message. If you're stumped, check the answer at the end of the chapter.

Poe was interested enough in codes and ciphers to write an essay on the subject entitled "A Few Words on Secret Writ-

ing." In that essay, he offered the substitution system shown in Figure 25. You can easily use it in your secret writing.

)	shall stand for		a
(	"	"	b
—	"	"	c
✱	"	"	d
.	"	"	e
,	"	"	f
;	"	"	g
:	"	"	h
?	"	"	i or j
!	"	"	k
&	"	"	l
o	"	"	m
'	"	"	n
†	"	"	o
‡	"	"	p
¶	"	"	q
☞	"	"	r
]	"	"	s
[	"	"	t
£	"	"	u or v
$	"	"	w
¿	"	"	x
¡	"	"	y
☜	"	"	z

Figure 25

Another writer of mysteries who used a cipher system in one of his short stories is Sir Arthur Conan Doyle (1859–1930), creator of Sherlock Holmes. In "The Adventure of the Dancing Men" (from *The Return of Sherlock Holmes*), Holmes solves a mystery by discovering that a string of stick figures really represents letters of the alphabet. Figure 26 shows you what Holmes and his trusty sidekick, Watson, encountered.

Figure 26

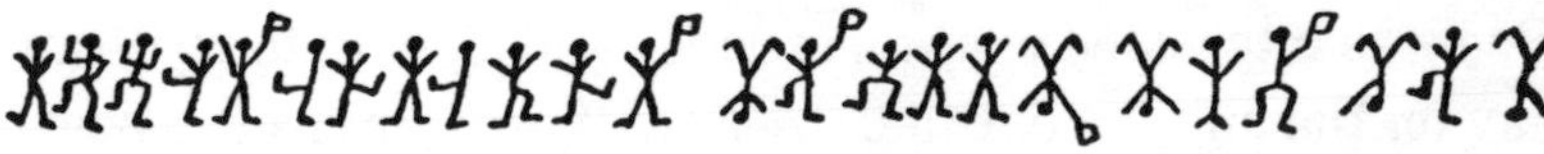

One substitution system uses the *typewriter* keyboard as an enciphering device. Instead of writing the letters of your plaintext, write the letters that appear immediately to their right on the typewriter keyboard. Figure 27 shows a typewriter keyboard.

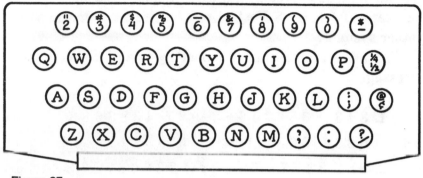

Figure 27

Using this system, decipher the message VPFRD SMF VO½JRTD STR IDRF S;; PBRT YJR EPT;F. Then try to come up with other systems for a typewriter cipher. Jot them down in your notebook and save them for future use.

The *telephone dial* can also be used for a cipher system. To encipher your message, all you have to do is substitute the

Figure 28

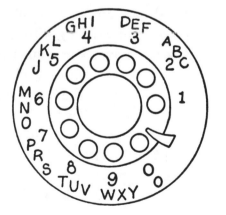

numbers on the dial for the letters. But each number stands for three letters! The number 4, for example, stands for G, H, and I. How would you indicate the letter you mean? You could easily draw a small line over the number, changing its direction for each of the three letters, so 4̀ would be G, 4́ would be H, and 4̂ would be I. Or you could use a dot as your indicator: T=·8, U=8̇, V=8·. Don't be afraid to come up with other systems.

Using the first telephone cipher system, decipher these messages:

1. 8̀4̀3̀ 8̀3̀5̀3̀7̀4̀6̀6̀3̀ 9̀2̀7̀ 4̀6̀8̀3̀6̀8̀3̀3̀
   6̀8̀3̀7̀ 6̀6̀3̀ 4̀8̀6̀3̀7̀3̀3̀ 9̀3̀2̀7̀7̀ 2̀4̀6̀.

2. 8̀4̀3̀ 3̀4̀7̀7̀8̀ 7̀8̀2̀5̀4̀2̀ 3̀3̀6̀6̀6̀7̀8̀7̀2̀8̀4̀6̀6̀
   6̀3̀ 8̀4̀3̀ 8̀3̀5̀3̀7̀4̀6̀6̀3̀ 9̀2̀7̀ 4̀3̀5̀3̀ 4̀6̀
   7̀4̀4̀5̀2̀3̀3̀5̀7̀4̀4̀2̀.

Since a good cryptographer must have a keen sense of observation, try this: Put your hand over the drawing of the telephone dial. Now, which two letters are *not* on the dial? (No peeking!) Can you think of some words you might want to use that contain either of these letters? Write a few in your notebook.

Before you can use the telephone dial substitution, you must overcome the problem of working without a Q and a Z. Any suggestions? Talk them over with your partner. There may be a number of words that require a Q, like quick, quiet, and quit. You're less likely to miss the Z, but words like zoo and puzzle might come in handy. For the Z you can simply use a zero. Finding a symbol for the Q might be more difficult, but you could use 7̲ or 7̶. Try it.

The most common cipher system is, oddly enough, the *Morse code*, developed by Samuel F. B. Morse and first

A •—	H ••••	O ———	V •••—
B —•••	I ••	P •——•	W •——
C —•—•	J •———	Q ——•—	X —••—
D —••	K —•—	R •—•	Y —•——
E •	L •—••	S •••	Z ——••
F ••—•	M ——	T —	
G ——•	N —•	U ••—	

Figure 29

demonstrated in 1837. Yes, if you recall the definitions of code and cipher, you will see that the Morse code is really a cipher! It is shown in Figure 29.

The best-known Morse code message is, of course, the SOS, an international signal of distress: ••• ——— •••. My first name would be:—— — •— —•• . What about your name? Encipher it in Morse code in your notebook. And, for additional practice, try deciphering this message: — •••• •• ••• •• •••
—• • •— —•• —•• ——— •— —•• •• ——• •••• • •—

Unlike other codes and ciphers, the Morse code can be communicated in several ways. Let's say your partner lives next door or on the other side of your back yard. With some practice, you could easily send your message by flashlight, making quick flashes for the dots and longer ones for the dashes. If the distance between you is shorter, you could use a simple telegraph key (see Appendix 2) to make buzzing sounds.

Another common way of communicating secret messages is with the *semaphore*, which is widely used by ships at sea. This is a system of visual signaling using two flags, one held in each hand. The semaphore symbols are shown in Figure 30.

The semaphore positions can be streamlined so that they look like the hands on a clock. With this in mind, try to come up with a substitution system, writing it in your notebook. I

Figure 30

have given you a few letters in Figure 31 to start off with.

After you have completed the modified semaphore chart, use it to encipher this message: THE SUN RISES IN THE EAST. Then try deciphering the message in Figure 32.

Figure 31

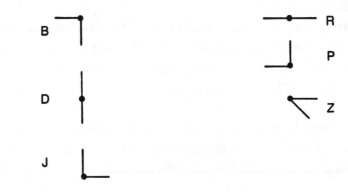

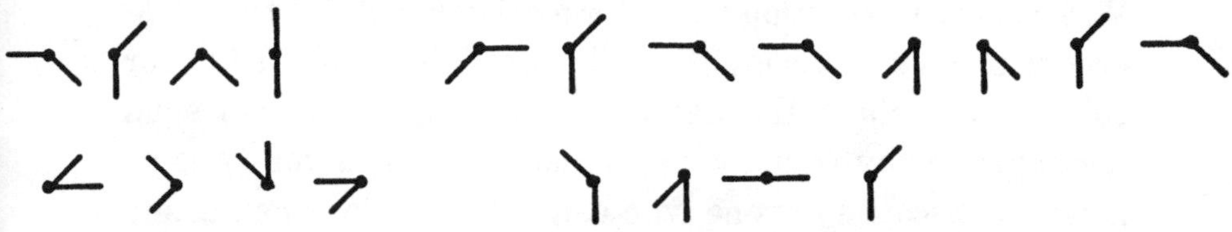

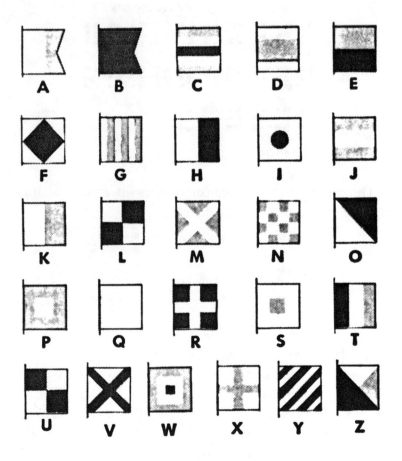

Figure 32

In addition to the Morse code and the semaphore system, ships use flags with colorful patterns to send messages. The *International Flag Code* uses the flags shown in Figure 33.

Figure 33

With some construction paper (or a selection of felt-tip markers), you can easily copy these designs. (See book jacket for color.) By flashing the flags one at a time, you can send messages to any friend who can see you. Be on your guard, however, because anyone who can see your flags can easily intercept your messages.

People who are blind often rely on a system of "writing" that could also serve as a substitution system for secret messages. *Braille,* as it is called, was developed in 1824 by Louis Braille. It consists of raised dots that, when touched, can be recognized as letters of the alphabet. The Braille alphabet is shown in Figure 34.

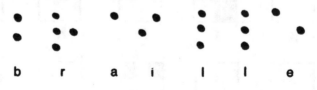

Figure 34

The name of the originator of this international form of writing would appear like this:

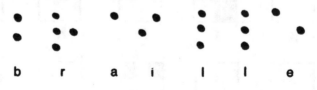

b   r   a   i   l   l   e

For practice, try enciphering this message: BRAILLE LOST HIS SIGHT IN AN ACCIDENT.

One cipher that has an especially interesting history is the *Rosicrucian cipher.* It is also known as the *Freemason cipher,* named after a secret society that used it. The cipher seems to go back to the time of the Crusades (1095–1272), but it wasn't used much after the sixteenth century. However, it became popular again in this country during the Civil War. In December 1863, when postal inspectors opened a letter addressed to a Confederate spy, they found a secret message written in the *pigpen cipher*, as it is most widely known. The pigpen cipher is shown in Figure 35.

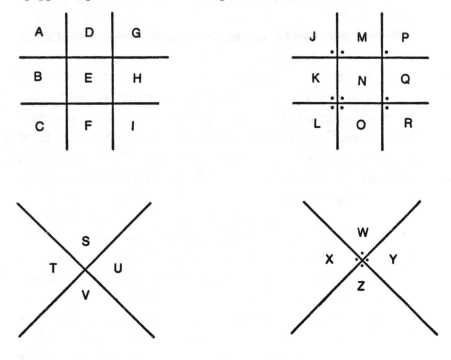

Figure 35

To encipher a letter, simply find that *part* of the diagram that corresponds to the letter you want to use. For example, A would be ⌟, B would be ⌟, and J would be ⌟. T would be > and Z would be ∧. The words PIGPEN CIPHER, for instance, would look like Figure 36.

Figure 36

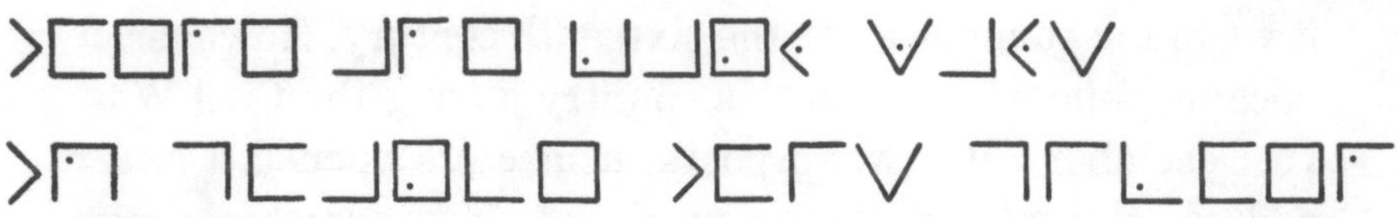

＞ＣＯＲＯ　ＪＲＯ　ＬＪＪＤＫ　ＶＪＫＶ
＞Ｎ　ＴＣＪＤＬＯ　＞ＣＲＶ　ＴＲＬＣＯＲ

Figure 37

How about a little practice? Decipher the message shown in Figure 37.

Notice that a single dot can distinguish one symbol from another, so be sure to include it when necessary. This system could be varied in many ways. For example, instead of starting with A in the upper left-hand corner of the first figure, you could place A in the lower right-hand corner and continue from there. Or you could put the dots in the first and third figures instead of in the second and fourth. I'm sure you can find other variations on this cipher. When you have come up with some good ones, write them down in your notebook.

Another early substitution alphabet was created at the end of the sixteenth century in England, at a time when different religious groups struggled for power. Queen Elizabeth I, a Protestant, felt so threatened by her Catholic cousin, Mary, Queen of Scots, that she held her captive in a castle.

Using a cipher system, Mary communicated with her friends on the outside. One of them, Gilbert Gifford, sneaked secret messages in and out of the castle in a beer keg. What Mary didn't know, however, was that Gifford was really an agent for Elizabeth. (The queen had over fifty spies throughout Europe!)

Slowly Elizabeth gathered information on her cousin's plot to assassinate her. Mary was brought to trial and convicted on the evidence of her secret messages; then she was beheaded.

Her substitution system used a symbol for each letter of the alphabet, as well as one for some common words. Her alphabet is shown in Figure 38.

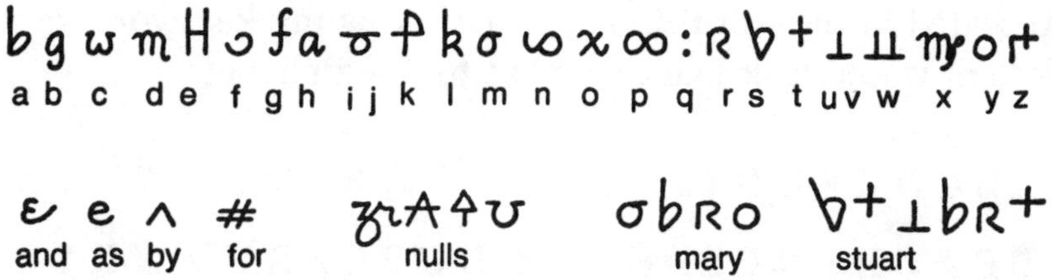

b g ш ɱ H ɔ ꞩ a ʊ ꝑ k ʊ ɯ x ∞ : R Ϸ + ⊥ ⊥⊥ ɱ o ɼ
a b c d e f gh i j k l m n o p q rs t uvw x yz

ɛ e ∧ #   ꝃ A ꝗ ʊ   ʊ b R o   Ϸ + ⊥ b R +
and as by for   nulls   mary   stuart

Figure 38

Mary, Queen of Scots, wasn't the only woman to lose her
life over secret messages. One of the most famous spies in
history by far was Mata Hari, a Dutch woman who was
arrested by the French in 1917 for carrying coded messages
for the Germans. British codebreakers, working out of their
famous headquarters called Room 40, were responsible for
decoding the secret messages that led to the capture of Mata
Hari. The woman claimed she was working as a double agent.
Although the facts surrounding her arrest are still unclear,
she was tried by a military court in Paris and executed by a
firing squad in the summer of 1917.

A more recent substitution system, shown in Figure 39,
was used by the Nazis during World War II.

a b c d e f g h i j k   n

o p q r s t u v w x y z

Figure 39

One variation of the Caesar cipher is the *mixed cipher*. In
it a key word is used to make the shift in the alphabet. The
key word should be at least five letters long, with no letter

[55]

repeated in the word. Using *teaching* as my key word, my letters would look like this, next to the alphabet:

A B C D E F G H I J K L M N O P Q R S T U V W X Y Z

T E A C H I N G B D F J K L M O P Q R S U V W X Y Z

Notice that I wrote the key word at the beginning of the alphabet and then filled in the remaining letters that did not appear in the key word. The letters that match up in the alphabet and the cipher will only help confuse outsiders. Can you think of other suitable key words? Write down some of them in your notebook to save for quick reference.

The substitution ciphers I have explained so far have one thing in common. They all follow a set pattern. In other words, one symbol always stands for the same letter of the alphabet. Let's look at a system that does not follow that pattern and is, therefore, more difficult to break.

The *date shift cipher* uses a date—any date—to determine the symbol for each letter. For our example, let's take November 26, 1922, the birthday of Charles Schulz, creator of Snoopy, Charlie Brown, and the other *Peanuts* characters. Another way to write that date is 11/26/22. Taking out the slashes, we have a six-digit number: 112622. That will be our key number. Now, let's take a message that we want to encipher: THE TRAIN WILL LEAVE AT ONE. We print out the message, then under it write the key number, repeating it as often as necessary:

THE TRAIN WILL LEAVE AT ONE.
1 1 2 6 2 2 1 1 2 6 2 2 1 1 2 6 2 2 1 1 2 6.

The number under each letter tells us how many places *forward* we must shift the letter to get the enciphered letter.

In other words, shift the T one place and we get U. The H we will move one place, giving us I. Moving E two places, we get G, and so on with the rest of the message.

You can see that a letter in the plaintext will probably not have the same symbol each time it is used. In our message above, the T is enciphered once as U, then as Z, then as U again. Our message would be enciphered like this: UIG ZTCJO YONN MFCBG CU PPK. Did you notice that when we moved the V forward six places, we had to go to the beginning of the alphabet again?

If you were born in a month and/or on a day with only one digit, simply place a zero before or after that digit. For instance, February 9, 1955, could be written 020955 or 209055. Be careful with October, which is the tenth month. Don't confuse it with 01.

Let's see if you can do it. Using my birthday, which is 072745, encipher the following message:

SECRET FILM WILL ARRIVE BY
072745 0727 4507 274507 27

COURIER TOMORROW.
4507274 50727450.

Write out your answer in your notebook.

Thomas Jefferson (1743–1826) designed a substitution cipher that is similar to the date shift cipher in that it assigns substitutions at random. A letter does not have the same cipher letter every time it is used. In fact, it may have the same cipher letter only by chance.

Jefferson's *cipher wheel* was a set of thirty-six wooden disks, roughly 1½ inches in diameter and perhaps ¼ inch thick. Each disk carried an alphabet in random order around its edge. The thirty-six disks were stacked together and held that way with a metal rod that ran through the center of each one, allowing room to turn the disks.

To encipher a message using a cipher wheel, you would merely line up the disks so your message appeared in one line. Then you could use *any other line* for your enciphered message. The person to whom you were sending the message would simply set his identical set of disks to the enciphered line, then skim over the other lines until he found the one that made sense.

With very little work, you can build two versions of Thomas Jefferson's cipher wheel with materials found around your house. Both wheels can be used to send secret messages, so give both of them a try.

Let's start with the disk version. Instead of working with wood and steel as Thomas Jefferson did, we'll use a sheet of blank paper (8½″ by 11″) and a tube from a roll of paper towels. You'll also need a ruler, scissors, a pencil, and some cellophane tape.

To begin, draw twenty-one lines at ½-inch intervals across the paper so that it looks like the lined paper you use in school. Next, draw twenty-six lines at 3/16-inch intervals down your paper. Then add one more line ¾ inch from the last one. After you've drawn the lines, turn your paper so the longer lines and skinnier spaces go across the page. Now comes the easy part. Starting in the space in the upper left-hand corner, print one letter of the alphabet in each box in that column. Do the same thing in all twenty-two columns. The final box in each column—the big one—will be blank, but don't worry about it.

Remember that last line you drew? Well, cut the paper in two along that line, and discard the part without letters on it. Your paper should now look like Figure 40, only much larger.

A	A	A	A	A	A	A	A	A	A	A	A	A	A	A	A	A	A	A	A	A	A	A
B	B	B	B	B	B	B	B	B	B	B	B	B	B	B	B	B	B	B	B	B	B	B
C	C	C	C	C	C	C	C	C	C	C	C	C	C	C	C	C	C	C	C	C	C	C
D	D	D	D	D	D	D	D	D	D	D	D	D	D	D	D	D	D	D	D	D	D	D
E	E	E	E	E	E	E	E	E	E	E	E	E	E	E	E	E	E	E	E	E	E	E
F	F	F	F	F	F	F	F	F	F	F	F	F	F	F	F	F	F	F	F	F	F	F
G	G	G	G	G	G	G	G	G	G	G	G	G	G	G	G	G	G	G	G	G	G	G
H	H	H	H	H	H	H	H	H	H	H	H	H	H	H	H	H	H	H	H	H	H	H
I	I	I	I	I	I	I	I	I	I	I	I	I	I	I	I	I	I	I	I	I	I	I
J	J	J	J	J	J	J	J	J	J	J	J	J	J	J	J	J	J	J	J	J	J	J
K	K	K	K	K	K	K	K	K	K	K	K	K	K	K	K	K	K	K	K	K	K	K
L	L	L	L	L	L	L	L	L	L	L	L	L	L	L	L	L	L	L	L	L	L	L
M	M	M	M	M	M	M	M	M	M	M	M	M	M	M	M	M	M	M	M	M	M	M
N	N	N	N	N	N	N	N	N	N	N	N	N	N	N	N	N	N	N	N	N	N	N
O	O	O	O	O	O	O	O	O	O	O	O	O	O	O	O	O	O	O	O	O	O	O
P	P	P	P	P	P	P	P	P	P	P	P	P	P	P	P	P	P	P	P	P	P	P
Q	Q	Q	Q	Q	Q	Q	Q	Q	Q	Q	Q	Q	Q	Q	Q	Q	Q	Q	Q	Q	Q	Q
R	R	R	R	R	R	R	R	R	R	R	R	R	R	R	R	R	R	R	R	R	R	R
S	S	S	S	S	S	S	S	S	S	S	S	S	S	S	S	S	S	S	S	S	S	S
T	T	T	T	T	T	T	T	T	T	T	T	T	T	T	T	T	T	T	T	T	T	T
U	U	U	U	U	U	U	U	U	U	U	U	U	U	U	U	U	U	U	U	U	U	U
V	V	V	V	V	V	V	V	V	V	V	V	V	V	V	V	V	V	V	V	V	V	V
W	W	W	W	W	W	W	W	W	W	W	W	W	W	W	W	W	W	W	W	W	W	W
X	X	X	X	X	X	X	X	X	X	X	X	X	X	X	X	X	X	X	X	X	X	X
Y	Y	Y	Y	Y	Y	Y	Y	Y	Y	Y	Y	Y	Y	Y	Y	Y	Y	Y	Y	Y	Y	Y
Z	Z	Z	Z	Z	Z	Z	Z	Z	Z	Z	Z	Z	Z	Z	Z	Z	Z	Z	Z	Z	Z	Z

Figure 40

Now cut out the twenty-two alphabet strips. Be careful, and try to cut as straight as possible. When you've finished cutting, tape each strip around the paper towel tube. Do it so that they turn easily on the tube, but do not move or interfere with the other strips.

Once you've taped all twenty-two strips in place, your Thomas Jefferson cipher wheel is ready to serve you as it served our third president nearly two hundred years ago.

The second version of the cipher wheel will be made of six circles of cardboard instead of twenty-two strips of paper. Each circle will be a little smaller than the one under it. Also, each circle will contain a complete alphabet. The process of enciphering and deciphering will be the same as with the disk version, except that the circles will have to be set several times, because you will be working with only six alphabets instead of twenty-two, and your message will almost always be longer than six letters.

For this project, gather together several pieces of 8½" by

11″ heavy paper or cardboard (the kind found at the bottom of a pad of paper), a compass, a protractor, a ruler, a strong pair of scissors, a pencil, and a brass paper fastener.

The first step is to measure and cut out the six circles. Using the compass, draw circles of these radii: 1 inch, 1½ inches, 2 inches, 2½ inches, 3 inches, and 3½ inches. This will give you six circles with diameters of 2 inches, 3 inches, 4 inches, 5 inches, 6 inches, and 7 inches.

When the circles have been cut out, you must divide each one into twenty-six sections, like the pieces of a pie. To do this, you must use your protractor to measure angles of fourteen degrees. It might sound difficult, but let me give you a hint that might make your work easier and more accurate.

On a separate sheet of paper, draw a line across the center of the page. Mark the midpoint of the line. Holding your paper so that the line goes from left to right, put the center point of your protractor on the midpoint of that line. Now, very carefully, mark off every fourteen-degree interval on the paper. Take your ruler and draw a line through each point you marked with the protractor and the midpoint of your center line. Go from one edge of the paper to the other, so that your paper looks like Figure 41 when you've finished.

Now you are ready to mark your circles. Do this by taking each circle and placing it on the paper in such a way that the tiny compass hole in the center matches the midpoint of the center line. Then simply draw across the circle the lines that are on the paper.

After you've marked all the circles, write the alphabet on the outer rim of each circle. When the circles are placed on top of one another, starting with the largest, they should look like Figure 42. (Note that the secret message in Figure 42 begins with the word *remember*. Since it's longer than six letters, even the first word doesn't fit in one setting!)

Next, use the sharp point of the compass (be careful!) to

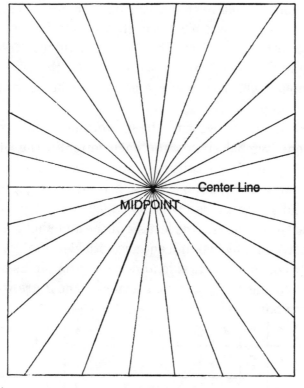

Figure 41

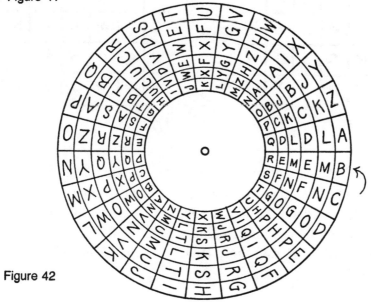

Figure 42

[61]

make a bigger hole in the center of each circle. Then press the brass paper fastener through the hole in every circle, starting with the smallest. The circles should turn freely, and each alphabet should line up with those on the other circles. Your cipher wheel is now ready to encipher and decipher your messages.

Up to this point, we have been working with systems in which one symbol stands for each letter in the plaintext. Another type of substitution cipher uses *two* symbols for each letter of the plaintext. These are called *polyliteral* systems, and generally use what is called the *Greek square*.

In the Greek square, the letters of the alphabet are written out in a five-unit by five-unit square with identifying numbers or letters down the left side and across the top as shown in Figures 43 and 44. Notice that letters *I* and *J* are written in the same box.

	1	2	3	4	5
1	A	B	C	D	E
2	F	G	H	IJ	K
3	L	M	N	O	P
4	Q	R	S	T	U
5	V	W	X	Y	Z

Figure 43

	A	B	C	D	E
A	a	b	c	d	e
B	f	g	h	ij	k
C	l	m	n	o	p
D	q	r	s	t	u
E	v	w	x	y	z

Figure 44

Each letter is then enciphered by the two-digit number that represents first the row (horizontal) and then the column (vertical) in which the letter appears. For example, my first name would be enciphered this way: P = 35, A = 11, U = 45, L = 31. Put together, PAUL would be enciphered as 35114531.

	1	2	3	4	5
6	A	B	C	D	E
7	F	G	H	IJ	K
8	L	M	N	O	P
9	Q	R	S	T	U
0	V	W	X	Y	Z

Figure 45

One variation of the Greek square is shown in Figure 45.

Using the grid in Figure 43, decipher the message below. I've separated each group of numbers into "words" to make things easier for you. However, there is no rule that says you must do this. Running the numbers together could make it more difficult for your enemy, should he or she intercept your message.

44 23 24 43   32 15 44 23 34 14   34 21

15 33 13 24 35 23 15 42 24 33 22   24 43

32 34 42 15   44 23 11 33   44 52 34   44 23 34 45 43 11 33 14

54 15 11 42 43   34 31 14.

Decipher this message, using the grid in Figure 44:

DC CE BD AE DC   CB AA ED   AB AE   AA CA CA

AA DB CD DE CC AD   ED CD DE.

After you have deciphered these messages, try enciphering your full name, using the grid in Figure 43.

There is no reason always to fill in the alphabet in the same manner as I have done. You could, for instance, start in the lower right-hand corner and work backward. Or you could start in the upper right-hand corner and go down one row and up the next. These are only two of the many possible variations. In your notebook, fill in a grid with a couple of variations.

Answers to Chapter 3

Translations of Caesar cipher, pages 42–43:

1. The Caesar cipher is very old.
2. Working with ciphers takes practice.
3. You can hide secrets with ciphers.

Translations using variations 3 and 5, page 44:

1. You may find this system more difficult than the other one.
2. Do not be a litterbug.

Translation of the message from "The Gold Bug," page 45:

"A good glass in the bishop's hostel in the devil's seat—twenty-one degrees and thirteen minutes—northeast and by north—main branch seventh limb east side—shoot from the left eye of the death's head—a beeline from the tree through the shot fifty feet out."

Translation of typewriter message, page 47:

Codes and ciphers are used all over the world.

Translations of telephone ciphers, page 48:

1. The telephone was invented over one hundred years ago.
2. The first public demonstration of the telephone was held in Philadelphia.

Translation of Morse code, page 49:

This is really a cipher.

Translation into modified semaphore cipher, page 50:

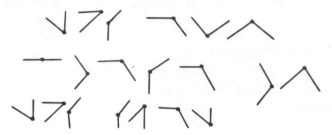

Translation of modified semaphore cipher, page 51:

Send messages with care.

Translation into Braille, page 52:

Translation of pigpen cipher, page 54:

There are many ways to change this cipher.

Translation into date shift cipher, page 57:

SLEYIY FPNT ANLS CYVNVL DF GTUYKLV
YOTQYVTW.

Translations of Greek square ciphers, page 63:

1. This method of enciphering is more than two thousand years old.
2. Spies may be all around you.

Chapter 4
Tables and Charts:
Transposition Ciphers

The *transposition cipher* is based on the simple idea of transposing, or rearranging, the letters of your plaintext to hide its meaning. This method of enciphering has one advantage over substitution ciphers. It does not require any fancy gadgets like Jefferson's cipher wheel or even a simple construction like the grille.

If you are familiar with the anagram, you know that it is a kind of transposition. The one significant difference between an anagram and a transposition is that the anagram makes sense. A message enciphered by means of transposition does *not* make sense. WAITRESS, for example, is an anagram for A STEW, SIR? THEY SEE is an anagram for THE EYES, and ONE HUG is one for ENOUGH. You could rearrange the letters in DESPERATION and get A ROPE ENDS IT.

On the other hand, if MCOE TA CENO was your enciphered message, you would decipher it by transposing the letters to find COME AT ONCE. WRBEEA FO HTE TTRRAIO would be deciphered as BEWARE OF THE TRAITOR. This gives you an idea of how transpositions work, although you will see that there are systems that make transposing a more organized system of secret writing.

Before we begin exploring transposition systems, try to decipher a few simple anagrams, working in your notebook. Remember to scramble the letters so that each one forms a new word.

1. CAT
2. GOD
3. TIME
4. TAR

Now try deciphering these short transposed messages:

1. EMET AIRTN TA NVSEE.
2. RECA CSSEEANYR.
3. RTBLEOU OSNO RFO UYO.
4. MNYEO STUM EB STEN.
5. EELF WNO.

One of the earliest transposition ciphers was the *skytale* (rhymes with *Italy*), designed nearly 2400 years ago by the Spartans of ancient Greece. It is a simple device that involves wrapping a narrow strip of paper around a slender rod and then carefully writing a message on the strip of paper, along the length of the rod. When the paper is unwrapped, the letters are transposed and the message enciphered.

To make your own skytale, you will need only a slender rod and a narrow strip of paper (about ½ inch wide). A pencil will serve nicely as the rod. To begin, wrap the strip of paper around the pencil evenly, leaving enough space between each turn to write one letter. Now carefully print your plaintext on the paper across the length of your pencil. When you get to the end of the paper, turn the pencil a bit and go on printing your message. Continue this procedure until your message is completed. If you have followed these instructions carefully, your skytale will look like the one in Figure 46.

Figure 46

Although only three lines of my message appear in the drawing, a complete message might take up all the space around the pencil. When you unfurl your message, you will have a narrow strip of paper with letters printed in a neat row.

You are now ready to send the enciphered message to your partner, who will wrap the strip of paper around his or her pencil and decipher it easily. There is one important thing to remember. Your partner must have a rod the same thickness as yours. If, for example, you use a regular pencil to encipher the message and he or she uses a thick one to decipher it, the letters will not line up correctly.

Another method of transposing is called the *rail fence cipher* because the letters are arranged to look like a split-rail fence. If you've ever taken a ride through the country or through farmlands, chances are you have seen this sort of fence, probably in pasture lands. Looking *down* on it, you would see this pattern:

Suppose you wanted to encipher this message: SEND MONEY TODAY. To do so, you would first write the letters of the plaintext in the pattern of the rail fence:

```
S   N   M   N   Y   O   A
  E   D   O   E   T   D   Y
```

Next, you would write out the letters in the top line, then the letters in the bottom line. So your enciphered message would be SNMNYOA EDOETDY. Isn't that easy! Just to make sure you really understand the rail fence cipher, try these practice messages:

1. SEND COURIER USUAL ROUTE.
2. EXTRA FUNDS AND GUNS NEEDED TODAY.
3. ESCAPE BLOCKED UNTIL FRIDAY.
4. DESTROY ALL CODE BOOKS AT ONCE.

By the way, there is no rule requiring you to transmit your enciphered message in two long "words." You could even divide these "words" into shorter ones to disguise the cipher you used. The message SEND MONEY TODAY could easily have been written as SNMN YOA EDOE TDY or SN MN YOA ED OE TDY. The only requirement, of course, is that you leave extra space to show your partner where the first line ends.

Before we go on to some more complicated transposition ciphers, try to decipher a few messages. Simply write one "word" above the other. Then read the letters, following the zigzag pattern of the rail fence.

1. MEASAINTON ETTTTOANO.
2. BWRODULAET EAEFOBEGNS.
3. TEERLTOWYTHDMSAE HRAEOSFASOIEESGS.
4. UDROEAETHVCUAE NECVRGNSAEORG.

Of course, there can be many variations of the rail fence cipher. For instance, you could reverse the order of your letters when you write out your enciphered message. You could do this in both rows or in only one. In another variation, you could use, let's say, three letters for the zigzag instead of two. HELP IS URGENTLY NEEDED would look like this:

```
H       I       G       L       E
   E  P  S  R  E  T  Y  E  D  D
      L     U     N     N     E
```

It could be written this way: HIGLE EPSRETYEDD LUNNE. Can you think of other variations of this system? When you come up with some, write them in your notebook. And remember, you can vary the system in any way you wish, as long as your partner knows what you've done.

Most transposition ciphers involve a path traced through a geometric figure of letters. These ciphers are called *route transpositions*. To illustrate one such system, let's use SEND MONEY TODAY SO WE CAN GO for our plaintext, and a square for our geometric figure. In a square with twenty-five places, print the plaintext, one letter per place. Start in the upper left-hand corner, go down one column, then the next, and so on for the five columns. Fill in any unused squares with nulls. Our completed square should look like the one shown in Figure 47.

S	O	O	O	N
E	N	D	W	G
N	E	A	E	O
D	Y	Y	C	T
M	T	S	A	R

Figure 47

Once we have completed the square, we are ready to encipher the message. To do that, we must decide which route we
will use. One simple path would be from left to right, beginning at the top. The enciphered message would then read:
SOOON ENDWG NEAEO DYYCT MTSAR. Or we could
follow rows 1, 3, 5, 2, 4 to encipher.

We could use other geometric figures. Let's encipher the
same message with a 3- by 8-place rectangle (see Figure 48).

S	Y	W
E	T	E
N	O	C
D	D	A
M	A	N
O	Y	G
N	S	O
E	O	T

Figure 48

Now our message, again taken from left to right, top to
bottom, would read: SYW ETE NOC DDA MAN OYG NSO
EOT.

There are three rules that you and your partner must
remember if your route transpositions are to be successful.

First, you must agree in advance on the size and shape of
the figure. The two figures we used above were just the right
size for the twenty-three-letter message. But we could as
easily have used three nine-place squares and enciphered the
message in three parts (see Figure 49).

S	D	N
E	M	E
N	O	Y

T	A	O
O	Y	W
D	S	E

C	G	V
A	O	E
N	A	T

Figure 49

The second rule to remember: You must agree on the starting point and the route your message will take in the figure. You can imagine what would happen if you enciphered the plaintext by starting in the upper left-hand corner and going down each column, but your partner thought you'd started in the bottom left-hand corner and gone up one column and down the next. To show you what I mean, look again at the message on page 72: SOOON ENDWG NEAEO DYYCT MTSAR. These "words" are rows 1, 2, 3, 4, and 5 of the square. Suppose your partner thinks you've written rows 2, 4, 1, 3, 5. What message would your partner get?

Finally, you must determine in advance the number of letters in each enciphered group. The number you select is up to you, as long as you and your partner agree. Look at Figure

50, in which a 6- by 4-place figure is used to encipher our original message.

S	M	Y	A	W	N
E	O	T	Y	E	G
N	N	O	S	C	O
D	E	D	O	A	T

Figure 50

With the simplest transposition, you could write the enciphered message in two ways:

1. SMYAWN EOTYEG NNOSCO DEDOAT.
2. SMY AWN EOT YEG NNO SCO DED OAT.

In his book *Cryptography: The Science of Secret Writing*, Laurence Dwight Smith shows forty different patterns of route transpositions! You will find a few in Figure 51, and you can check Smith's book for others. Begin "reading" each figure at letter A and follow through the alphabet.

Figure 51

S	T	U	V	W	X
R	Q	P	O	N	M
G	H	I	J	K	L
F	E	D	C	B	A

A	B	D	G	K	O
C	E	H	L	P	S
F	I	M	Q	T	V
J	N	R	U	W	X

A	B	C	D	E	F
P	Q	R	S	T	G
O	X	W	V	U	H
N	M	L	K	J	I

U	T	M	L	E	D
V	S	N	K	F	C
W	R	O	J	G	B
X	Q	P	I	H	A

What are some other route transposition patterns? How about writing a few possibilities in your notebook. And while you're at it, draw a few geometric figures that you could use besides a 6- by 4-place rectangle and a 5- by 5-place square.

If you'd like to make your transpositions more difficult to break, there is a method that uses a key word to confuse. Let's take a simple message: COURIER LEAVES AT SEVEN. Put it into a 5- by 4-place grid, starting in the lower left-hand corner and going up each column (see Figure 52).

R	L	E	S	N
U	R	V	T	E
O	E	A	A	V
C	I	E	S	E

Figure 52

The key word must be a five-letter word with no letters repeated. Let's use PLATE. Next, assign each letter a number according to its alphabetical order:

$$P \quad L \quad A \quad T \quad E$$
$$4 \quad 3 \quad 1 \quad 5 \quad 2$$

Now write the number above your pattern so each column is numbered (see Figure 53).

$$(P \quad L \quad A \quad T \quad E)$$
$$4 \quad 3 \quad 1 \quad 5 \quad 2$$

R	L	E	S	N
U	R	V	T	E
O	E	A	A	V
C	I	E	S	E

Figure 53

The numbers tell you the order in which you will write each column when you send your message: EVAE NEVE LREI RUOC STAS.

Let's say you were sending the enciphered message to me. I would know, of course, that the key word is PLATE. So I would figure out the five-digit number and place it above an empty grid. Then I would simply fill in each column according to the key numbers, placing the first "word" of the message in the column headed by the number 1 (see Figure 54).

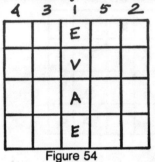

Figure 54

I would then continue with the other four "words." After I had filled in the first three "words," the grid would look like the one shown in Figure 55.

4	3	1	5	2
	L	E		N
	R	V		E
	E	A		V
	I	E		E

Figure 55

It would now take me only a minute to complete the message.

You may ask yourself: Why bother with a key word when all you really need is a five-digit number? Well, you probably will find it easier to remember a five-letter word than a five-digit number.

Other suitable key words are YOURS, WORDS, OTHER, AFTER. Write ten good key words in your notebook. Remember, each word must have five letters with no letter repeated.

Anagrams, page 68:

1. act
2. dog
3. mite
4. rat

Translations of transpositions, page 68:

1. Meet train at seven.
2. Care necessary.
3. Trouble soon for you.
4. Money must be sent.
5. Flee now.

Translations into rail fence cipher, page 70:

1. SNCUIRSARUE EDOREUULOT.
2. ETAUDADUSEDDOA XRFNSNGNNEETDY.
3. ECPBOKDNIFIA SAELCEUTLRDY.
4. DSRYLCDBOSTNE ETOALOEOKAOC.

Translations of rail fence cipher, page 70:

1. Meet at station at noon.
2. Beware of double agents.
3. There are lots of ways to hide messages.
4. Undercover agents have courage.

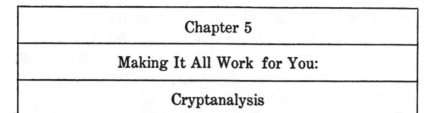

Chapter 5
Making It All Work for You:
Cryptanalysis

Now that you've learned how to design and send codes and ciphers, you're ready for the detective work. In this chapter you'll learn how to crack a secret message. While it will require some new skills, don't forget all you've learned so far, because knowing how to build secret messages will help you take them apart. It will take some luck, true, but it will also take good old-fashioned thinking, the stuff Sherlock Holmes called "elementary." You'll have some false starts and you'll run down some blind alleys, but if you stick with it, you'll be able to attack a message and crack it without much trouble.

Before we get down to some serious *cryptanalysis*, or the process of breaking codes or ciphers, let me say a few words about breaking codes. It is extremely difficult to break a code. It takes training and experience that none of us has. If you look at the sample from the code book in Chapter 1, you will see that there is really no connection between one column and the other. That's one reason codebreaking is much harder than cracking a cipher. In ciphers there are established patterns that will help you, but in codes there are no such patterns. So let's leave codebreaking to the experts and spend our time on something that will give us some fun instead of a headache.

The first thing to do after you have intercepted a message is make a *letter-frequency chart.* This is simply a chart that shows which letters in the message are used most often. It will tell you whether you are working with a transposition cipher or a substitution cipher. Without that answer, you can't begin your detective work.

A frequency chart is easy to make. Just write the alphabet down the left-hand margin of a sheet of paper. Then go through the message letter by letter. Every time a letter appears in the message, put a small line next to that letter on the chart. When you've gone through the entire message and filled in the frequency chart, you can look for that first important clue.

The frequency with which letters are used varies from language to language. In English, for example, the five most commonly used letters are: E, T, A, O, N. This means that in a random sample from an English book, there will be more E's than any other letter. The letter T will be the next most frequently used letter, and so on. Here are the five most frequently used letters in five other languages:

German: E, N, I, R, S
French: E, A, I, S, T
Spanish: E, A, O, S, N
Portuguese: A, E, O, R, S
Italian: E, A, I, O, N

Here is the complete *frequency list* for English:

E, T, A, O, N, I, S, R, H, L, D, C, U,
F, P, M, W, Y, B, G, V, K, Q, X, J, Z

I suggest that you memorize this list, because you will refer to it every time you begin your attack on an intercepted message. If you memorize it, you will be able to work more quickly, since you won't have to refer to a book or list.

Once you've made a frequency chart for the intercepted message, compare it with the frequency list for English. If they are similar, you can assume you have a transposition cipher on your hands. In other words, someone has taken a message and simply rearranged the letters. If the frequency chart and list are not similar, figure you're working on a substitution cipher. Someone has substituted less frequently used letters for more frequently used letters. Naturally, if your message contains numbers, signs, or assorted strange symbols, you will know that you're working with a substitution.

Suppose you discover that you're trying to crack a substitution cipher. What then? Well, *if* your message follows the usual pattern of the English language, the rest should be pretty easy. So, let me show you how cryptanalysis works.

The first thing to do is find the most frequently used letter and assume that it stands for E. Wherever that letter appears in the message, write in an E. Next, do the same thing with the second most frequently used letter. Write in a T wherever that letter appears in the message. Remember that these are *guesses*, perhaps educated guesses, but guesses nonetheless. If your guesses are correct, however, at this point you've deciphered about twenty-five percent of the message, because E and T make up about a quarter of the letters used in the English language. If you can identify the next three letters on the frequency list (A, O, N), you've deciphered forty percent of the message.

Once you've substituted E, T, A, O, and N for the five most frequently used letters in the message, you should begin looking for words that are familiar. For example, if you see a three-letter word that starts with T, what word will it most likely be? THE. What about a three-letter word that begins with A? AND. If you see a single letter, what will it probably be? A, rather than O or I. As you fill in the letters, your message will crack slowly, like an egg.

That's how it should work. Before I give you an example to illustrate the theory, here are some important frequency lists. Keep them in your notebook for future reference, as they will help you to break substitution ciphers.

Most Frequently Used Four-Letter Words

1. that	11. been
2. with	12. good
3. have	13. much
4. this	14. some
5. will	15. time
6. your	16. very
7. from	17. when
8. they	18. come
9. know	19. here
10. want	20. just

Most Frequently Used Three-Letter Words

1. the	6. not
2. and	7. had
3. for	8. her
4. are	9. was
5. but	10. one

11. our		16. can	
12. out		17. day	
13. you		18. get	
14. all		19. has	
15. any		20. him	

Most Frequently Used Two-Letter Words

1. of	11. he
2. to	12. by
3. in	13. or
4. it	14. on
5. is	15. do
6. be	16. if
7. as	17. me
8. at	18. my
9. so	19. up
10. we	20. an

Most Frequently Used First Letters

T, O, A, W, B, C, D, S, F, M, R,
H, I, Y, E, G, L, N, P, U, J, K

Most Frequently Used Last Letters

E, S, T, D, N, R, Y, F, L, O, G,
H, A, M, P, U, W

Most Common Double Letters

SS, EE, TT, FF, LL, MM, OO

Now let's see how it all works. Here's the intercepted message:

IAAP IA WP PDA YKNJAN KB JEJPD WJZ IWEJ
WP OARAJ PKIKNNKS JECDP. XNEJC AOYWLA
LHWJO WJZ YKZA XKKG.

First of all, make your frequency chart. For this message, it will look like this:

A / / / / / / / / / /
B /
C / /
D / / /
E / / / /
F
G /
H /
I / / / /
J / / / / / / / / / /
K / / / / / / / /
L / /
M

N / / / / /
O / / /
P / / / / / / /
Q
R /
S /
T
U
V
W / / / / / / /
X / /
Y / / /
Z / / /

The first thing you should see is that you are working with a substitution. You should know this because your frequency chart does not follow the English frequency list. If you were working with a transposition, E would have been the most frequently used letter.

Once you realize you have a substitution, what next? Print out the enciphered message, leaving enough space between the lines to write in your educated guesses. It is a good idea to write the message in one color ink and the plaintext in another. This could save you from getting confused.

Write out the alphabet on a separate piece of paper. This will be your working alphabet. Next to each letter, you will write the letter that has been substituted for it. As you figure out what more and more letters stand for, you should see some patterns develop in the working alphabet.

In our message, A and J are the most commonly used letters. Let's assume that A is E. We can make that assumption for two reasons. First of all, A comes before J in the alphabet, so that is a logical place to start. Second, we see that the first word of the message contains a double letter combination, a good bet to be EE. So write E above each A in your message, then E next to the A in your working alphabet. The message will look like this:

```
  E E     E           E           E
_____
I A A P  I A  W P  P D A  Y K N J A N  K B

                                E   E
_____
J E J P D  W J Z  I W E J  W P  O A R A J

_____
P K I K N N K S  J E C D P  X N E J C

E           E                       E
_____
A O Y W L A  L H W J O  W J Z  Y K Z A X K K G
```

Are there any words that you can recognize after you've written in the E's? What about PDA? Check your chart of most frequently used three-letter words. Which ones end with E? Which is the most common? THE. Write in TH and fill in T and H above every P and D. Then put P next to T in your alphabet, and D next to H. Even at this early stage of deciphering your message, you can see that some patterns and words are emerging:

```
  E  ET    E     T  THE          E
  I  AAP   IA   WP  PDA   YKNJAN  KB

      T H                T     E    E
  J E J P D   W J Z   I W E J   W P   O A R A J

  T                        H T
  P K I K N N K S   J E C D P   X N E J C

  E          E                             E
  A O Y W L A   L H W J O   W J Z   Y K Z A X K K G
```

Next, take a look at the first word in your message. What
letter must I stand for? The first word could be BEET, but
that would make the next word BE. I think we can take an
educated guess that the first two words of the message are
not BEET BE. It is much more likely that I stands for M.
That would give you MEET ME for your first two words.
Make sense? Okay, write in M wherever you see I, and put
it next to the I in your alphabet.

About this time you should be getting a good feeling.
Slowly but surely, like the petals of a flower, the message is
beginning to open for you. Notice that we have not been
using the frequency chart. We did for the first letter, but
after that we played our hunches. And we can be pretty sure
that we have broken four letters: A = E, P = T, D = H, and
I = M.

Move on to the third word. It looks promising. Logically,
what two-letter word that ends with T will follow MEET ME?
It couldn't be IT; that doesn't fit. Check the list of Most
Frequently Used Two-Letter Words for a word that ends
with T and would make sense here. AT. To check it out, note
that there are seven W's in the message, which makes W the
third most frequently used letter. Isn't A third on the English
frequency list? Great. Wherever you see a W, write in an A.
And don't forget to fill in your working alphabet.

```
M E E T   M E   A T   T H E                 E
I A A P   I A   W P   P D A   Y K N J A N   K B

          T H   A         M A        A T      E   E
J E J P D   W J Z   I W E J   W P   O A R A J

T   M                     H T
P K I K N N K S   J E C D P   X N E J C

E     A E       A       A               E
A O Y W L A   L H W J O   W J Z   Y K Z A X K K G
```

Doesn't that open up some interesting possibilities! Look at them all! Scan your message to see if there are any immediate discoveries. Of course there are. The most common three-letter word that begins with A is AND. So wherever you see a J, write in an N, and wherever you see a Z, write in a D. Things are really shaping up.

```
M E E T   M E   A T   T H E                 N E
I A A P   I A   W P   P D A   Y K N J A N   K B

N   N T H   A N D   M A   N A T      E   E N
J E J P D   W J Z   I W E J   W P   O A R A J

T   M                 N       H T             N
P K I K N N K S   J E C D P   X N E J C

E     A E       A N       A N D         D E
A O Y W L A   L H W J O   W J Z   Y K Z A X K K G
```

I think it's time to bust this message wide open. If you look at the alphabet you've been keeping, you should see two interesting spots:

```
W     Z A     D       I J             P
a b c d e f g h i j k l m n o p q r s t u v w x y z
```

The important spots are, of course, *de* and *mn*. You can see that D = Z and E = A. This seems to indicate that you're working with a Caesar cipher that begins at E, runs to the end of the alphabet, and then ends at D. The fact that M = I and N = J seems to give strength to our deduction. Now, if you write in the rest of the alphabet, you should see that our guess was right on the money. The proof, of course, is that the letters we have already figured out—A, H, and T— fit into place perfectly. Beautiful work! Now go back to your message and fill in the other letters. Message broken.

Do you get the idea behind the process? We started by making a frequency chart and assuming that the most frequently used letter was E. Once that was filled in, we looked at the message for clues rather than following the chart blindly. We played a hunch or two, made an educated guess or two. The rest was easy. However, we did use the frequency chart to support our clever guesses.

There is one thing you must understand. The frequency charts are based on averages. That means not every letter in every message will follow the charts perfectly. Almost all of ours, in fact, did not. That is why you shouldn't rely on the chart totally and should try, instead, to make as many educated guesses as possible.

Now for some practice. Remember the hints and suggestions I've given you, and try to break these ciphers:

1. MAX MBFX YHK RHNK XLVTIX BL GHP.
   EXTOX TM LXOXG YHEEHP KHNMX MH MAX
   LXT VAXVDIHBGM.
2. QCF QSJBW NBYY IF FJSYL. LVP JSF QV IF
   BW HJS VWF RFJQ WBWF. GFUJSQ JQ GJNW.

How about one more? This one is a little scary, but don't panic. Handle the numbers just as if they were letters.

3. 3-10-22 6-22-18-20 16-15-20-22-16-8 7-20 10-8-11-15
   20-21-15 26-21-10-4-15 12-16-10-25-15-11-20 23-18 23-8
   13-7-8-19-15-16 23-17 3-10-22 18-20-7-3 7-26-7-3
   11-7-4-4 6-15 7-8-3 20-23-6-15.

The ciphers you've been working with have all been substitutions. But suppose you could tell from the frequency chart that you had a transposition. What then? Well, you would follow another method of attack, one that would work for you as well as the method you used for breaking the substitutions.

Let's say you intercept this message: CEOOIH AANUVO LSAAEU LSSRAS MOYRTE. What will you do with it? Right. The first thing to do is make a frequency chart. When you have done that, you will learn that this is a transposition cipher. Another hint that it might be a transposition is the fact that all the "words" are the same length.

After you have discovered that you are working with a transposition cipher, I suggest that you thumb back to Chapter 4 and review what you have learned about transpositions. The most important thing to remember is that this type of cipher usually follows a route traced through a geometric pattern of letters. The first thing to do, therefore, is try to find the correct geometric table. Since this message contains thirty letters arranged in five six-letter "words," try a 6- by 5-place table. Always try the easiest, most obvious possibility first.

When you set up the message in a 6- by 5-place table, you'll get this:

```
C E O O I H
A A N U V O
L S A A E U
L S S R A S
M O Y R T E
```

Can you find the message in this block of letters? Sure you can. One thing I'm sure you saw was the word HOUSE down the fifth column. Further inspection should show you that the message starts in the upper left-hand corner and goes down each column in order. Simple? Though not all of the transpositions will be this simple, this will give you the idea behind deciphering one.

There are several things that I could have done to this message to make it a little more difficult. I could have rearranged the "words" to form this message: CEOOIH LSAAEU MOYRTE AANUVO LSSRAS. That would simply follow a 1-3-5-2-4 pattern. I could have written out the message starting with the bottom "word" and moving up the grid. Or I could have used a 5-3-1-4-2 pattern.

Time for practice. I'll give you a message and tell you the size of the pattern. You see if you can put all the "words" in the right order and crack the cipher.

1. (3×10) IER TVS HEE INE NLA KLB TAL HHE ASE TIP.
2. (7×5) ENENALL TMRAHLU SYDNSHA ICLDUEP LHIYOAR.
3. (5×5) GYRBW IRDRA VESOY EGTAZ MAODN.
4. (7×4) BTOURRC EHOTAPO OEKFPLW NLOOUEZ.

Before you try to break a cipher that you know is a transposition, determine how many geometric tables are possible with the number of letters in the message. For instance, in example 2 above, there are thirty-five letters. That means there are only two possible patterns: 7 by 5 and 5 by 7. But there are more possibilities for example 1, with its thirty letters: 2 by 15, 15 by 2, 3 by 10, 10 by 3, 5 by 6, and 6 by 5.

You must be aware of all possibilities before you begin looking for a solution, because to find it you may have to try every one.

Next, look on the table for combinations like TH, THA, and so on. Such combinations are called *digraphs* and *trigraphs*. Finding them could give you just the lead you are looking for. Here are some of the most frequently used digraphs and trigraphs.

Frequently Used Digraphs:

TH, ER, ON, AN, RE, HE, IN, ED, ND, HA, AT, EN, ES

Frequently Used Trigraphs:

THE, AND, THA, ENT, ION, TIO, FOR, NDE, HAS, NCE, EDT

Finally, remember that the "words" in the message do not necessarily indicate the shape of your grid. Six-letter words, for example, could really be made up of two three-letter "words." Along these same lines, don't assume that the "words" follow one another as they are printed in the message. Exercise 1 on page 90 could have been written to follow a 1-3-5-7-9-2-4-6-8-10 pattern, or a 2-4-6-8-10-1-3-5-7-9 pattern. That's why you have to be ready to shift "words" around and look for common letter combinations.

You can see that the more familiar you are with transposition ciphers, the easier it will be for you to break them. Are you ready to try your hand at a few secret messages? You won't have to figure a frequency chart because you know these are all transpositions.

1. ITCBNOY LOHORXB OWTSEPA VAHTDLL
   ETEOSAL.
2. INDS EAWE NEAH JKLC OIKA YBIE RYNB
   IMGE DGOH INNT.
3. ITBF HAYF ACTU VYHD EAEC ARNA SGAM
   MLMF ALEO.

If you had any trouble with example 3, just remember that
the words may not be written in the order in which they go
on the grid. Also, remember that there are over forty possible routes through a grid, so don't give up if the first two or
three do not work out for you.

Some final advice on breaking ciphers: Take your time
when you're working on a message. Don't be afraid to make
an educated guess or play a hunch, but don't jump to conclu-
sions. Don't be a slave to the frequency charts, but keep them
handy, because they will help you. If you get stuck, look over
this chapter, as well as the ones on substitutions and transpositions. And try practicing with your friend, because giving
each other messages to crack will help you.

Answers to Chapter 5

page 84:

> Meet me at the corner of Ninth and Main at seven
> tomorrow night. Bring escape plans and code book.

pages 88–89:

1. The time for your escape is now. Leave at seven. Follow route to the sea checkpoint.
2. The train will be early. You are to be in car one, seat nine. Depart at dawn.
3. You must return at once. The whole project is in danger if you stay away. Call me any time.

page 90:

1. I think that I shall never see a bleep.
2. Listen my children and you shall hear Paul.
3. Give my regards to Broadway.
4. Be on the lookout for a purple cow.

page 92:

1. I love to watch the Boston Red Sox play ball.
2. I enjoy riding my bike and walking on the beaches.
3. I have a small gray cat by the name of Macduff.

Appendix

Appendix 1				
How to Make				
Different Grilles				

To make a grille other than the one in Chapter 2, you will need the supplies that you used earlier: a pen or pencil, a ruler, a hobby knife, tracing paper, and some 3″ by 5″ file cards. Remember to be careful when you cut. Your fingers cut much more easily than a file card. And always do your cutting over a piece of cardboard.

First of all, place a piece of tracing paper over the pattern shown in Figure 56. Then draw on it the outline of the card and any six or eight boxes that do *not* have the same number.

Figure 56

15	14	13	13	14	15	
12	11	10	10	11	12	
9	8	7	7	8	9	
6	5	4	4	5	6	
3	2	1	1	2	3	
3	2	1	1	2	3	
6	5	4	4	5	6	
9	8	7	7	8	9	
12	11	10	10	11	12	
15	14	13	13	14	15	

For the grille in Chapter 2, you may remember that we used boxes 13, 9, 1, 5, 7, and 15. It's not necessary to skip a line between windows, but the grille is easier to use if the windows have a little space between them. You can see that your grille can have a maximum of fifteen windows. However, it will work better if you limit it to six or eight windows.

Now cut out of the tracing paper and card the boxes of your choice. Then clip a corner. That's important because it gives you a point of reference when you flip the grille. Remember, it doesn't matter how you first flip the grille, as long as you flip it four ways.

Using Figure 56, you should be able to make many different grilles.

Appendix 2
How to Make
a Telegraph Key

With a minimum of expense, it is possible to build a telegraph key
that will allow you to send secret messages in Morse code from one
room in your house to another. It is even possible to extend such
a system from one house to another, provided, of course, you have
enough wire to cover the distance between the houses.

To build a telegraph key, you will need:

1. A six-volt lantern battery. Buy the type with screw
   terminals and plastic nuts. This will allow you to attach
   wires easily.
2. A buzzer. An electrical supply house or a hardware store
   will carry this item. Get the cheapest one you can.
3. A doorbell push button.
4. Twenty-four inches of bell wire.
5. A scrap piece of wood, about 8″ by 10″. Any kind of
   wood will do.
6. Tools: screwdriver, strong pair of scissors.

Once you've collected all your materials, you are ready to con-
truct your Morse code telegraph key.

Step 1. Position the battery, the buzzer, and the button on the board in the pattern illustrated in Figure 57. If your piece of wood is smaller than 8″ by 10″, don't worry. Simply move the parts closer together.

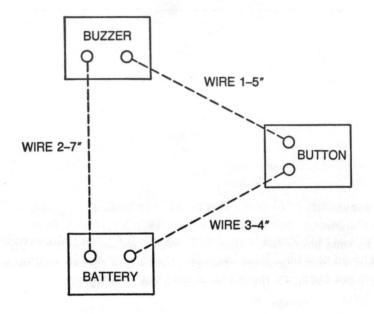

Figure 57

Step 2. Cut the three pieces of bell wire that will connect the parts of your key. Follow the diagram in Figure 57 for proper lengths. After you have cut the wire, strip about ¾ inch of the plastic insulation from each end of each piece of wire. To do this, cut through the insulation (without cutting the wire), then simply pull it off the end of the wire. Be careful not to cut your fingers. You might want to get some help with the stripping from an adult.

Step 3. Attach one end of Wire 2 to one of the battery terminals. It doesn't matter which one. Just wrap the wire around the terminal and hold it in place with the plastic nut. Next, remove the cover of the buzzer and attach the other end of Wire 2 to one of the terminal screws in the buzzer. You will have to loosen the screw, wrap the wire around it, then tighten it again.

Step 4. Attach one end of Wire 1 to the other terminal screw in the buzzer.

Step 5. Attach one end of Wire 3 to the other battery terminal.

Step 6. Attach the other end of Wire 1 to one of the terminal screws on the underside of the button. Attach the other end of Wire 3 to the other terminal screw in the button.

Step 7. Now take a few minutes to attach the button and buzzer to the scrap piece of wood by inserting screws through the extra holes in each and turning them into the wood. You might find it easier to drive in your screws if you make a starter hole with a nail or awl. It is also a good idea to tape your battery to the board with masking tape.

If you have followed these directions carefully, your Morse code key should now buzz loud and clear when you press the button. If it does not buzz, try these troubleshooting steps:

1. Check your battery. Make sure it is not run down or dead.
2. Recheck each step in the directions. Have you done everything correctly?
3. Check each point where contact is made. Make sure that all wires are properly stripped and tightly secured.

If you and your friend want to send messages from one room to another or from one house to another, you will, of course, need two buzzers, two buttons, one battery. You will also need enough wire to connect the two keys. When you have everything you need to make the keys, you must wire your keys according to the diagram in Figure 58.

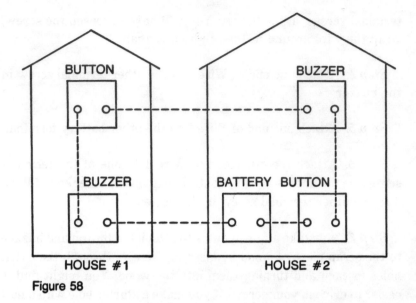

Figure 58

Appendix 3

How To Disguise

Your Secret Messages Further with Invisible Inks

Invisible inks are a great method of sending secret messages. What's more, they will amaze your friends. With almost no effort at all, you will be able to make writing appear on a piece of paper that seems to be blank.

Certain fruit and vegetable juices make excellent inks. Citrus fruits—oranges, grapefruits, lemons—work well. So does apple juice. Even onion juice will make an excellent ink—if you don't mind shedding some tears while you're mashing up the onion! All of these juices can be used directly, without dilution. Since they will spoil if they're left out of the refrigerator for too long, it would be a good idea to put them in baby-food jars, then store them in your refrigerator. It would also be wise to label the jars so your family knows what's in them.

You can also use a sugar-and-water solution as an invisible ink. Just dissolve a teaspoon of sugar in a glass of water. A teaspoon of honey in a glass of water will work much the same way.

Soft drinks, like Coke and Pepsi, will work because of their sugar content. However, because of the coloring in the soda, you might have to dilute it with a little water. This is tricky. You'll have to run a few experiments to find the right combination of soda and water. After you've used a soft drink successfully, repeat the message using a *diet* soft drink. You will find that artificial sweeteners aren't always suitable substitutes for sugar!

If you dilute a teaspoon of regular table salt or Epsom salts (the stuff you use when you soak a sprained ankle) in a glass of water, you'll get a good ink. You can do the same with a solution using bicarbonate of soda. Straight white vinegar also works well.

There's one more item you can use to make invisible ink. That is the styptic pencil, the short, chalklike stick your father may use when he cuts himself shaving. If your dad doesn't have one, you can buy an inexpensive one in a drugstore. Dab a little water on the end (do *not* put it against your tongue!) and use it like a crayon.

It will probably take a little practice to use these inks correctly, especially because your writing instrument will have to be a quill, a toothpick, or a small paintbrush. Perhaps you'll feel uncomfortable writing with these, but stick with it. In a short time you will be able to write with an invisible ink without soaking the paper or leaving other telltale marks.

All of these inks can be developed by exposing your message to some heat. A large light bulb (150 to 200 watts) is a good, safe source of heat. How do you use heat to develop your message? When you have written out your message and given it a chance to dry, all you have to do is hold it close to the light bulb. Do not let it touch the bulb, or you will char your piece of paper. Hold it just close enough so you can feel the heat on your fingers. Try five or six inches. That should work. If it doesn't, carefully move your paper a little closer to the light bulb. When the paper becomes warm, your message will appear. It's that easy.

Index